"If you... will b...

Santiago g... to his men. They moved to stand one on either side of Bolan, gripping his arms and moving him across the cell to stand in front of a closed door on the far side. Santiago himself reached to free the bolts that held the door shut. He grasped the handle, ready to open it.

"In Miami you caused us a great deal of trouble. A number of our people died because you refused to back away. You made it clear you would refuse to stop searching for Maggie Connor. Congratulations, you have found her."

Santiago pushed the door, then stepped aside so the Executioner could be shoved toward the opening.

It was another cell. A cold and hostile place.

Bolan was staring at Maggie Connor. Or what was left of her.

MACK BOLAN®
The Executioner

#295 Hostile Alliance
#296 Nuclear Game
#297 Deadly Pursuit
#298 Final Play
#299 Dangerous Encounter
#300 Warrior's Requiem
#301 Blast Radius
#302 Shadow Search
#303 Sea of Terror
#304 Soviet Specter
#305 Point Position
#306 Mercy Mission
#307 Hard Pursuit
#308 Into the Fire
#309 Flames of Fury
#310 Killing Heat
#311 Night of the Knives
#312 Death Gamble
#313 Lockdown
#314 Lethal Payload
#315 Agent of Peril
#316 Poison Justice
#317 Hour of Judgment
#318 Code of Resistance
#319 Entry Point
#320 Exit Code
#321 Suicide Highway
#322 Time Bomb
#323 Soft Target
#324 Terminal Zone
#325 Edge of Hell
#326 Blood Tide
#327 Serpent's Lair
#328 Triangle of Terror
#329 Hostile Crossing
#330 Dual Action
#331 Assault Force
#332 Slaughter House

#333 Aftershock
#334 Jungle Justice
#335 Blood Vector
#336 Homeland Terror
#337 Tropic Blast
#338 Nuclear Reaction
#339 Deadly Contact
#340 Splinter Cell
#341 Rebel Force
#342 Double Play
#343 Border War
#344 Primal Law
#345 Orange Alert
#346 Vigilante Run
#347 Dragon's Den
#348 Carnage Code
#349 Firestorm
#350 Volatile Agent
#351 Hell Night
#352 Killing Trade
#353 Black Death Reprise
#354 Ambush Force
#355 Outback Assault
#356 Defense Breach
#357 Extreme Justice
#358 Blood Toll
#359 Desperate Passage
#360 Mission to Burma
#361 Final Resort
#362 Patriot Acts
#363 Face of Terror
#364 Hostile Odds
#365 Collision Course
#366 Pele's Fire
#367 Loose Cannon
#368 Crisis Nation
#369 Dangerous Tides
#370 Dark Alliance

Don Pendleton's The Executioner
DARK ALLIANCE

A GOLD EAGLE BOOK FROM
WORLDWIDE.

TORONTO • NEW YORK • LONDON
AMSTERDAM • PARIS • SYDNEY • HAMBURG
STOCKHOLM • ATHENS • TOKYO • MILAN
MADRID • WARSAW • BUDAPEST • AUCKLAND

If you purchased this book without a cover you should be aware that this book is stolen property. It was reported as "unsold and destroyed" to the publisher, and neither the author nor the publisher has received any payment for this "stripped book."

Recycling programs for this product may not exist in your area.

First edition September 2009

ISBN-13: 978-0-373-64370-7

Special thanks and acknowledgment to
Mike Linaker for his contribution to this work.

DARK ALLIANCE

Copyright © 2009 by Worldwide Library.

All rights reserved. Except for use in any review, the reproduction or utilization of this work in whole or in part in any form by any electronic, mechanical or other means, now known or hereafter invented, including xerography, photocopying and recording, or in any information storage or retrieval system, is forbidden without the written permission of the publisher, Worldwide Library, 225 Duncan Mill Road, Don Mills, Ontario, Canada M3B 3K9.

This is a work of fiction. Names, characters, places and incidents are either the product of the author's imagination or are used fictitiously, and any resemblance to actual persons, living or dead, business establishments, events or locales is entirely coincidental.

® and TM are trademarks of the publisher. Trademarks indicated with ® are registered in the United States Patent and Trademark Office, the Canadian Trade Marks Office and in other countries.

Printed in U.S.A.

Where there is no vision, the people perish.
—*Proverbs* 29:18

When leaders are motivated by personal gain their vision becomes clouded and the people they are meant to protect instead suffer. I will make those men see the error of their ways.
—Mack Bolan

THE
MACK BOLAN

LEGEND

Nothing less than a war could have fashioned the destiny of the man called Mack Bolan. Bolan earned the Executioner title in the jungle hell of Vietnam.

But this soldier also wore another name—Sergeant Mercy. He was so tagged because of the compassion he showed to wounded comrades-in-arms and Vietnamese civilians.

Mack Bolan's second tour of duty ended prematurely when he was given emergency leave to return home and bury his family, victims of the Mob. Then he declared a one-man war against the Mafia.

He confronted the Families head-on from coast to coast, and soon a hope of victory began to appear. But Bolan had broken society's every rule. That same society started gunning for this elusive warrior—to no avail.

So Bolan was offered amnesty to work within the system against terrorism. This time, as an employee of Uncle Sam, Bolan became Colonel John Phoenix. With a command center at Stony Man Farm in Virginia, he and his new allies—Able Team and Phoenix Force—waged relentless war on a new adversary: the KGB.

But when his one true love, April Rose, died at the hands of the Soviet terror machine, Bolan severed all ties with Establishment authority.

Now, after a lengthy lone-wolf struggle and much soul-searching, the Executioner has agreed to enter an "arm's-length" alliance with his government once more, reserving the right to pursue personal missions in his Everlasting War.

Colombia

Mack Bolan heard them coming for him again. The same two men had taken him from his cell for the past two days, always at dawn. He recognized the familiar scrape of boots on the worn stone slabs.

He lay on his hard cot, counting the steps until they reached the cell door. Then came the grating of rusty bolts and the dry squeal of hinges as the door was pulled open. Pale light from the exterior passage lit the windowless cell. Each time they returned him to the room and closed the door he was plunged back into darkness.

Bolan swung his legs off the cot and stood, working the stiffness from his bruised limbs. He moved around as much as possible during the empty hours, resisting the urge to simply be still. He knew if he did that his battered body would seize up. Moving was no less painful, but he persisted, always thinking ahead to the moment when he would be offered his chance. He would be ready.

The first man to enter the cell was the one named Ricco. He was a big man, Bolan's height, but with a poor physique. Overweight and out of condition, he wore a permanent scowl on his unshaven dark face. A mass of thick, untidy black hair hung to his rounded, soft shoulders.

"Come on, yanqui," he ordered. His English was slow and heavily accented. "Your friend is waiting for you. Today is special, too."

He pushed the Executioner out of the cell ahead of him.

Ricco's partner, Noriamo, stood outside the cell. Noriamo was lean, his bony face scarred with knife marks. He wore a heavy mustache that hid his mouth. As Bolan passed him Noriamo watched with small, glittering eyes. His amusement at Bolan's nakedness was evident as he looked the captive over. As always, Noriamo was armed with a 9 mm Uzi that dangled from his skinny neck by a braided leather sling. He was constantly touching the weapon, as if to convince himself it was still there. Noriamo displayed a heightened degree of nervousness.

They walked the length of the passage, reaching another door. Noriamo slid past Bolan and pushed the door open. Bolan knew what to expect in the interrogation room—stone walls and rough concrete floor. The room was marked with dark, dried bloodstains that announced it had been used many times. Some of that blood was his own. He expected the same treatment as the day before, and the day before that. Brutal, but not life threatening. Punches and blows delivered by experts who knew how to inflict pain without killing the recipient. Beatings that went on for long periods until his numb face and body didn't register pain any longer. When that happened they stopped and let him rest before starting again.

And then the questions. Again and again. The same questions every time....

Who are you?

Who do you work for?

What do you know about us?

Bolan had no answers for them. They wanted confirmation of their suspicions about Maggie Connor. The detail Bolan had learned in Miami would stay with him until he was able to use it against them.

His chief tormentor, the man known as Santiago, was waiting for him.

The cell door closed with a solid thud.

"I admire your resilience," Santiago said quietly. "But as I have already said many times, you are simply wasting your life and my time. We can end the unpleasantness now. Give me what I want and it will be over very quickly. There's no point in letting this go on. In the end, you are going to die. Why prolong your suffering? Tell me what I need to know and when I tell Manolo he will order your death."

Bolan raised his head, matching Santiago's stare, defying the man's attempt at intimidation.

"I wouldn't tell you what day it is even if I knew."

Santiago's face darkened. He failed to conceal his anger at the American's open defiance in front of his men. This was how it had been since the man he knew as Matt Cooper had been brought here. If Santiago had been allowed to exhibit any compassion for him he might have because the big American had proved his will was strong enough to see him through this ordeal. But Santiago was under pressure to get the man to talk and his superiors were impatient.

"Cooper, you will give me what I want today. If you do not cooperate this will be the day you die. I want to show you something that will convince you I am serious."

Santiago gestured to his men. Each moved to either side of Bolan, gripping his arms and pulling him across the cell to stand in front of a closed door on the far side. Santiago himself reached to free the bolts that held the door shut. He grasped the handle, ready to open it.

"In Miami you caused us a great deal of trouble. A number of our people died because you refused to back away. You made it clear you would refuse to stop searching for Maggie Connor. Congratulations, Cooper, you have found her."

Santiago pushed the door, then stepped aside so the Executioner could be shoved toward the opening.

It was another cell. A cold and hostile place.

Bolan was staring at Maggie Connor. Or what was left of her.

Bolan saw, wanted to deny the evidence, but let it soak into his mind.

"You want to join her? That can be easily arranged if you refuse to speak to me. I will hang you on a hook next to her while you still live."

Santiago's soft words penetrated the white hot buzz that was rising inside Bolan. He knew he had to act within seconds.

"Bring him over here," Santiago snapped. "If he refuses to talk we will have to persuade him to change his mind."

Bolan felt Noriamo and Ricco grip his arms tightly as they moved him away from the open door. He offered no resistance, feigning weakness, head sagging. They turned him around. Santiago stood in the center of the cell, flexing hands that were encased in leather gloves. Slowly he reached beneath his coat and drew out a knife. It had a slim blade. Santiago stood waiting, savoring a cigar, until Bolan was dragged close enough for him to use his blade.

Turning his head slightly, Bolan saw the Uzi hanging from Noriamo's skinny neck.

He planted both bare feet down hard, hauling himself to a dead stop. His action caught the handlers off guard and allowed him to break from their already loose grips. He half turned to his right and head butted Ricco full in the face.

The guard's crushed and broken nose suddenly gushed blood. As he stepped away from Bolan he failed to see the American's hard swerve to the left and behind the dazed Noriamo.

Bolan's arms encircled the man's lean torso and gripped the dangling Uzi. He brought the weapon up to put Santiago in his line of fire and triggered it. Brass shell casings chinked as they hit the floor.

Santiago spun, his chest erupting in a mess of blood and shredded clothing. He screamed as he tumbled to the floor. The sound stopped when a second burst ended his life. The Executioner dropped the Uzi and gripped Noriamo's head with his powerful arms. Noriamo had no time to protest before Bolan snapped his neck. Bolan turned back to the stunned Ricco, who was still reeling from the savage blow that had smashed his nose. He grabbed the man's shoulders and spun him around. He looped his arm across Ricco's neck and hauled him off balance. As Ricco fell back, Bolan dropped, bracing himself on one knee. He slammed Ricco across his rigid thigh. The force was enough to snap his neck and Bolan pushed him to the floor.

It had taken no more than a few intense seconds. But

it was enough to end the lives of three men so that the Executioner could continue the mission that had started with Maggie Connor. He thought about what he'd learned.

Stony Man Farm, Virginia

"MAGGIE CONNOR HAS FED me information more than once," Hal Brognola said. "She's a damn fine investigative journalist. She's also one of the most generous people I know. Okay, she wants her story but if she comes across information that might help stall an injustice she passes it along. Her tips have always pointed us in the right direction."

"A journalist with a conscience," Bolan said.

"I can't knock that, Striker. She's helped Justice break a couple of hot investigations."

"What's the difference this time?"

"Maggie has been working an in-depth probe into the illegal supply of weapons to one of the cartels operating in and around Valledupar."

"That's cowboy territory," Bolan said.

The border territory between Colombia and Venezuela was a haven for smuggling of all kinds, from automobiles to electrical goods to drugs. Valledupar was the pivotal spot, where deals were done and the local gangs operated with impunity.

"Maggie told me she'd stumbled across details of a nasty operation. She gave me the bare bones because it was all she had at the time. Seems her Colombian subjects were having meetings with a couple of Cubans. Maggie was sure these guys were in government. She had managed to get some photographic evidence. She was being tight with what she told me. I think she was frightened, and that wasn't like her. Maggie is tough. She doesn't scare easily and she isn't reckless," the big Fed said.

"You guessed there was more to it?"

"Yes. But all she mentioned were the Colombians and the Cubans."

"How did you leave it?"

"Maggie said she was on her way back home. She said she'd contact me after she followed up a couple of leads here."

"Did she?"

"Once to say she was back and to wait for her to call again."

"But she didn't?"

Brognola shook his head. "I gave it a couple of days, then called her. Nothing. Maggie is *never* away from her cell phone. I had Bear run a trace on it. He finally locked on to the signal. It was weak but still active. I had Miami-Dade P.D. check it out. They located her car at the Miami airport, parked in one of the passenger lots. Maggie's cell was in the glove box."

Brognola handed a file to Bolan. "The cops ran more checks across the state. They came up empty. When they went to her Miami home her housekeeper said she was on an assignment. She hadn't been in touch but that was normal. Cops said they'd keep Maggie on file but there wasn't much more they could do."

"She's disappeared and you're thinking the worst," the Executioner said grimly.

"Striker, you and I know how these perps work. They'll go to any lengths to protect themselves and their territory. We've both seen what they do to anyone who poses a threat. If Maggie crossed the line and they picked up on it she would become a target."

"Hal, she could already be dead," Bolan said.

"I know. But if she has some information about these people they might have snatched her to force it out of her." Brognola hit the table with his fist.

"If that's the case she'd be better off dead."

"I know that," Brognola admitted. "But she could still be alive. I can't ask for official help because I've protected Maggie's identity. It was a one-to-one arrangement. I want it to stay that way until I'm satisfied no one had a trace on her."

"You think there's a leak?"

Brognola was in a delicate position. He suspected there was a break in department security that might have compromised Maggie Connor's safety. Bolan saw the look in his old friend's eyes. Brognola was caught in the middle. Wanting to protect his source. Determined to expose any covert activity within the Justice Department. Bolan understood the big Fed's dilemma.

"You don't need to ask, Hal. Let me read the file. I'm on board."

MAGGIE CONNOR'S HOME was in a quiet residential district that lay east of Miami's historic Biscayne Boulevard.

The reporter's home, smaller than some, was still spacious. Bolan swung his rented SUV off the road and came to a stop at the closed gates. He checked the grounds. Pristine. Empty. There was no movement. That wasn't unusual in itself. The occupants, if they were home, could be inside the house, or in the backyard.

Bolan's knowledge that Maggie Connor was missing gave him reason to think otherwise. He checked the gates. They weren't locked. He pushed them open and drove through. Once inside he returned to close the gates behind him, then drove up to the house.

He stood beside the SUV, his hand sliding inside his jacket to loosen the Beretta 93-R. His presence did not seem to have alerted anyone. At the front door he tested the handle. He wasn't surprised when the door opened, moving on smooth, balanced hinges. Bolan toed it fully open, drawing the 93-R. The entrance hall was bright from the sunlight streaming through numerous windows.

The Executioner stepped inside, his Beretta sweeping back and forth as he checked the area. He closed the door behind him, pausing to turn the lock. It was a reflex action to prevent anyone entering behind him.

Standing in the center of the hall Bolan strained to pick up any sound. Nothing.

He moved across the hall, up a couple of steps that led into a spacious living room. It was airy and filled with light from the floor-to-ceiling windows. Now he heard a soft, constant buzz of faint sound. As he turned to check the room the buzzing heightened. Sunlight picked up every detail in the room.

Papers and books were scattered across the floor. The drawers of a desk were empty, either lying on the rug or hanging crookedly from their runners.

Bolan saw the sprawled body, half stripped of clothing, exposed flesh showing where a knife had been used to cut and slash. Blood had run and pooled around the body. It had soaked into the carpet and partially dried. As Bolan stepped closer he picked up the smell of putrefying flesh and saw the black flies on the body. This had happened some time ago. Even from where he stood Bolan knew the dead woman was not Maggie Connor. Her file had given her height as five foot ten. The dead woman was much shorter. And she had blond hair, matted with blood. Maggie Connor had jet-black hair.

Bolan scanned the room thoroughly. The perpetrators had been looking for Maggie, or whatever they thought she knew. The woman on the floor had clearly been tortured for that information. If she had given her tormentors any information they could well be one step ahead in the search for the missing journalist. Or already have her in their hands.

As the Executioner turned away he spotted an object on the carpeted floor. He crouched to inspect it. It was the crushed remains of a thick cigar. He picked it up and sniffed the shredded leaves. He studied the rich, sweet aroma. He was certain he would recognize it again if he came across it.

He moved quickly and ran a full inspection of the house. All the other rooms had been subjected to thorough and destructive searches.

In the master bedroom he found the second and third bodies. One male, one female. Both had been tortured in the same fashion as the woman downstairs. The bodies showed signs of savage beatings and severe knife wounds. The off-white carpet beneath the bodies was caked with dried blood. More was spattered around the area. As before, the cloying smell of death hung in the warm air, and flies rose and settled as Bolan approached.

They were young and Hispanic. Bolan guessed they were probably Maggie Connor's house staff.

Back on the landing Bolan took out his phone and called Hal Brognola on a secured line.

"Not looking good," Bolan said. He told Brognola exactly what he had found. "They were looking for something. No way of knowing if they got it. The house staff were in the wrong place at the wrong time."

Bolan heard the big Fed's sharp intake of breath. "No sign of Maggie?"

"Nothing."

"Either she's on the move, or they've already picked her up."

"That's the way I see it. Hal, if she was on the run I would have expected her to contact you."

"Yeah, I know," Brognola said. "Are you still at the house?"

"I'm leaving now. Give me time to get out of the area, then call it in. Let the Miami P.D. do their thing and look after the victims."

"Will do. Striker, what the hell are these people after?"

"I'll tell you as soon as I find out."

Bolan recalled some information he had found when reading Maggie's file back at Stony Man Farm. Paul Sebring had worked with Maggie years back as her photographer. They had operated out of Central America, covering revolutions and military operations, bringing back hot reports and images. Then Sebring stepped away from the war zones and opened a photography studio in Miami. According to her file, Maggie and Sebring were still close and she sometimes used him to look after material she sent in from foreign assignments.

Bolan left Maggie's house and headed back in the direction of the city.

2

Luis Costa swirled the rich, dark rum around the glass, the telephone cradled against his ear. He took a swallow, letting the aromatic flavor of the liquor fill his mouth.

"Did he call the police?" he asked his lieutenant.

"I don't think so. He was inside for some time, so he must have found the bodies. When he left he closed the gates behind him. Like he didn't want to show he had been there."

"Did you recognize him?" Costa asked.

"Never seen him before. Big *hombre*. Looks like he could handle himself. Maybe an associate of the Connor bitch. Another journalist, maybe?"

"What are you doing about him?"

"I had people follow him back into the city. We took the details of his SUV. Cabrerro is running a check as we speak."

"Good. Watch him. See where he goes."

"What do you think?"

"I think we need to deal with him. But first we have to find out if Connor gave him any of the information she has been gathering. Use whoever you need to learn what you can. Remember, we have to contain this. If information leaks the whole operation could fall apart."

Costa dropped the phone back on its cradle, swiveling his chair around to stare out the window of his Miami office. He looked across the placid blue water of the bay, watching power boats race back and forth, leaving white trails behind them.

The man who had visited the Connor house intrigued him. It was the calm way he had exited the house and driven off. Calling in the police and waiting for them to arrive would have been the normal way to handle the situation, but for unknown reasons this man had withdrawn quietly, leaving the house as he had found it.

What did that mean?

Costa was determined to find out. As Raul Manolo's right-hand man, he had to inform his boss of this latest development.

His call was answered immediately.

"We have had an unknown visitor at the Connor house. I am having him checked out. Once we establish who he is we can decide what to do about him."

"A cop? Federal agent?" Manolo asked.

"That's what I'm trying to establish."

"Could he have been given Connor's findings?"

"Possibly. We won't know until we establish his identity."

"Just kill him," Manolo said.

"Shouldn't we first find out if he knows anything? In case he has passed any information along."

"This is fucking ridiculous. How many people do we have to deal with until we're sure we have things contained?"

"Let me deal with this. After all, it is what you are paying me for," Costa soothed.

"Keep me in the loop. But make your own decisions.

I have other things to deal with." Manolo slammed down the phone.

Costa's lieutenant called half an hour later.

"Cabrerro ran down the SUV through the rental agency. He tried a background check on the company that rented it. Nothing. He ran into serious encoding. No way can we find out who this *hombre* works for."

"What about *him?*"

"Same. No background details. It's like he just appeared out of nowhere."

"Keep checking." Costa considered what he had just heard. "Tomás, be ready to pull this guy off the street. We can't afford to have him poking around too much."

"Just give the word and he's ours."

"We need him alive, Tomás. He can't tell us anything if he's dead."

Costa opened a drawer in his desk and took out a cell phone. He dialed one of three special numbers. The man on the other end of the phone was an American.

"We have encountered an unexpected visitor. He was seen entering and leaving the Connor house. Didn't wait around." Costa recited the license plate number of the SUV his people had seen. "We can't find anything about him, or who rented the vehicle. He could be a nuisance. Use your police contact to identify him."

"I'll see what I can do. What have you done about him?"

"At the moment, I am keeping him under surveillance. I want to see what he does."

"Don't let him run on a long leash. If he gets lucky your troubles might get bigger."

"Don't think I haven't considered that," Costa muttered as he disconnected the call.

THE EXECUTIONER WAS in South Beach.

Paul Sebring ran his business from the top floor of a low-rise building. The street level was a seafood restaurant. Access to Sebring's office was via the wide alley that ran along the side of the building. White-painted steps led to the studio setup. Bolan made his way into a reception area with the walls covered in examples of Sebring's work. Even a cursory glance told Bolan the man was good. Behind the desk a pretty young woman glanced up from her computer keyboard.

"Hi," she said. "Can I help?"

"I need to speak to Paul Sebring," he said. "It's urgent."

"Okay," the woman said. She pointed at a door to one side of the desk. "Through there. Paul's office is on the left. Third door."

Bolan nodded. "Thanks."

As he walked along the corridor a door opened and a man leaned out.

"I'm Paul Sebring. Is there a problem?"

Bolan followed the photographer into a spacious, airy office that was expensively decorated and looked out over South Beach.

Sebring was a tall, fit-looking man in his midthirties. He was dressed in casual clothing and his pale blond hair was thick. He held out a large hand, smiling at his visitor.

"Matt Cooper," Bolan said. He showed Sebring his Department of Justice credentials and watched the man's expression grow serious.

"Now you have me worried."

They sat facing each other across Sebring's large desk.

"Maggie Connor," Bolan stated simply and watched Sebring's reaction.

"Is she okay?"

"That sounds as if you know she might be in trouble," the Executioner said.

"I never could hide my feelings. Look, all I can tell you is the last time she contacted me, Maggie...well, she sounded stressed. I've known her a long time and she isn't easily rattled."

"Did she tell you what was getting to her?"

"Not straight out. I just guessed it had to do with her current investigation. Something about illegal weapons dealing in Colombia. I told her she was on pretty thin ice with something like that. Those people do not play nice." Sebring stared hard at Bolan, trying to read his thoughts. "Jesus, is she hurt? Missing?"

"Looks that way. That's what I'm trying to find out. Did Maggie leave anything with you? Send you anything?"

Sebring sat upright, color draining from his face. He pushed up out of his chair and crossed the office, sliding open a drawer in a filing cabinet. He took out a small padded envelope.

"This arrived the other day. Never gave it much thought. Maggie's always sending me stuff to hold for her. She isn't much of an organizer."

Sebring offered the envelope to Bolan. He checked the postmark. It had been sent four days ago. Mailed from upstate Florida. He tore the sealing strip and tipped the contents out on Sebring's desk. There were two items. A digital camera memory card and a computer flash drive.

"I wonder what's on them," Sebring said.

"I'll know when I read them."

"No, you won't," someone said.

The Executioner turned and saw a broad-shouldered man in light pants and a colorful shirt. The thug had long black hair, pulled back in a ponytail, and a taut, angular face. There was a large pistol in the man's hand. It had a sound suppressor screwed on to it and the muzzle was pointing at Bolan. Behind the gunman was a second guy, dark and squat. He had Sebring's receptionist held tight against him, one hand clamped over her mouth, his other arm around her waist.

"Just give me the pieces," the gunman said.

Sebring exploded with anger. "Who the fuck do you think you are?"

The man didn't blink. He shifted the muzzle of the pistol and fired. The slug smashed into Sebring's left shoulder, knocking the surprised photographer backward.

Bolan swiveled from the waist, his right forearm sweeping around to catch the shooter's arm and deflect the pistol. Continuing the swift move Bolan brought his left arm up and circled the gunman's wrist. He trapped the arm beneath his own, clamping it to his side, swung hard and hauled the man off balance. Bolan grabbed for the pistol, twisting it brutally, snapping the finger still inside the trigger guard. The gunman let out a shout of pain and dropped the pistol. Bolan pivoted, the point of his right elbow thudding hard into the man's face. His nose broke under the impact. Blood began to gush from his nostrils. Bolan grabbed the man's hair and pulled his head forward and down. His rising knee met the gunman's forehead. The impact sent him reeling across the office, moaning, his hands clutched to his smashed face. Bolan spotted the dropped gun and scooped it up.

Satisfied that the man was out of action Bolan turned in the direction of the second intruder who was still holding Sebring's receptionist. The stocky man seemed stunned to see his downed partner curled up on the floor of the office. He turned his attention back to Bolan, now holding the pistol and closing the distance between them with speed. In a split second decision he released the receptionist, pushing her at Bolan, then turned and ran for the exit.

As the Executioner strode through the reception area he was only a couple of steps behind the fleeing figure. He raced through the door and caught the man at the top of the exterior steps. The man half turned in Bolan's direction as he sensed his pursuer's close proximity. His hand came out of his pocket to reveal a knife. The Executioner slammed the pistol across the side of the man's face. The blow was delivered hard, opening a raw gash. The thug squealed, an odd, high-pitched sound, and dropped the knife. The squeal trailed off as Bolan hit him a second time. The man stepped back, trying to avoid the blow. He moved too far and stepped over the edge of the top step. He tumbled down the steps, turning over a couple of times before hitting the bottom where he lay motionless.

Bolan returned to Sebring's office. He found the photographer slumped on the floor beside his desk, a bloody hand clutched to his shoulder. The receptionist was on the phone, calling for assistance. When she saw the gun in Bolan's hand her eyes widened in alarm.

He put the gun away. "Take it easy," he said. "I'm on your side."

He crossed to check the gunman. The man was still clutching his face, moaning softly. Then he went back to Sebring. The photographer, pale-faced and sweating, glanced up at the Executioner.

"You always bring guests to the party?" he asked.

"Never invited ones," Bolan said grimly.

"Next time, Cooper, just bring a bottle."

The receptionist put the phone down. "Police and ambulance are on their way."

Bolan turned to her. "Got any towels we can use to stop the bleeding?"

The young woman nodded and left the office.

"This has to do with Maggie?" Sebring asked.

Bolan took the items from the envelope and dropped them into his pocket. He glanced at Sebring. The photographer sensed what Bolan was silently asking and gave a brief nod.

The receptionist came back with some towels. She helped Bolan get Sebring into his chair. The Executioner wadded one of the towels and placed it over the wound.

"Hold that in place, miss."

She nodded and said, "The name's Carrie."

"Just keep good pressure on that towel, Carrie."

Bolan crossed to the door, taking out his phone. He punched in his contact number for Brognola. When the big Fed answered Bolan calmly explained what had happened.

"I can't walk out until Miami P.D. arrive. There's one perp on the floor and another outside the building. I won't leave and put these people in the way of further harm."

"When they arrive let me speak to the head honcho. I'll square things," Brognola said.

"Thanks."

"Any good going to come out of this?" Brognola asked.

"I don't know yet but tell Bear to get ready because I'm going to send him some information."

"Okay. Get back to me for your get-out-of-jail-free card."

Ten minutes later the office was a busy place. Police and paramedics vied for space. Sebring was given treatment prior to hospital transport to have the bullet removed from his shoulder. The gunman Bolan had put down was cuffed before his own ride for treatment. He'd said nothing, mostly due to the fact that his jaw was shattered and his nose badly crushed. The second attacker had vanished by the time the cops arrived. He had left blood behind on the concrete at the bottom of the steps but he'd disappeared. Carrie sat on a chair in one corner of the office, absently rubbing at the bloodstains on her dress but physically unharmed.

The Executioner stood to one side, waiting while the cop in charge had his conversation with Brognola. The cop ended the call and returned Bolan's phone to him.

"Looks like you're off the hook, Agent Cooper," he said amiably.

Lieutenant Gary Loomis was a lean, tanned cop in his thirties. His boyish face belied the things he had seen during his tenure with the Miami-Dade force. Despite the heat he wore a suit and tie. He stood in front of Bolan, hands on his hips, studying the big man.

"So what brought you to Sebring's office again?" the cop asked.

"Just following up on information received," Bolan recited. "An ongoing investigation. Sebring was pegged to answer a couple of questions. He isn't a suspect."

"Yeah, yeah," Loomis said. "Need to know and all that crap."

"Sorry, Loomis. If I could tell you more I would."

Loomis grinned. "Hell, don't sweat it. I got enough local crime to keep me busy. Last thing I need is another pile of paperwork to wade through. That yahoo you gave us is going to use up a whole tree's worth of forms by the time we get him processed."

"Any idea who he is?"

Loomis shook his head. "Maybe when we run his prints we'll get lucky."

"I'd appreciate hearing about anything you turn up."

Loomis handed Bolan a card. "Call me."

"Thanks."

"Anything for the Feds, Agent Cooper."

"SO WHERE TO NOW?" Brognola asked.

Bolan was behind the wheel again, heading out of the city. His only lead was the origin of the package Maggie Connor had mailed to Sebring.

"Riba Bay. Have Bear check the place out. See if there's anything Maggie might have been interested in. And tell him I'm going to download the contents of the memory card and flash drive as soon as I can."

Bolan ended the call.

He saw a shopping mall and eased off the highway, taking a parking spot close to the entrance. He made his way through the mall until he saw a computer store. Inside he asked for the manager. When the man arrived, looking all of sixteen years old, Bolan showed his Justice identification and explained what he wanted. Minutes later he was seated at a work station in the manager's office, downloading the memory card and flash drive to send to Aaron "the Bear" Kurtzman, the communications expert for Stony Man Farm. An acknowledgment e-mail came through saying the material had been received. Bolan erased it. He found the store manager, thanked him for his cooperation and returned to his SUV.

He had been driving for just under thirty minutes when he spotted the car tailing him....

The Executioner was at least an hour from Riba Bay. All he had to go on was the postmark on the package Maggie Connor had sent to Sebring. It was hardly much in itself, but it wasn't the first time Bolan had started out with almost nothing. But now he had company.

He spotted the tail car again in his review mirror, watched it as it narrowed the gap and kept edging closer.

Too close.

He checked the road ahead. For the past few miles he hadn't seen another vehicle. The road was clear in both directions. Bolan checked that his seat belt was secure, then hit the gas pedal and sent the big SUV surging forward. The force pushed Bolan back in his seat. He saw the tail car recede.

That wouldn't be the end of it, Bolan knew.

He was on a straight road, with no discernable turnoffs. There was no way out of this, except to keep driving and wait for something ahead to change things.

That *something* did show up a few miles along the road. But not in the way Bolan had hoped. He saw a distant configuration spanning the blacktop. At the speed he was traveling it only took a short time before he was able to identify it.

A full-size fuel tanker was stopped across the width

of the road, blocking it completely. The road on either side dropped away into drainage ditches, offering no avenue of escape.

The tail car was coming up behind him, relentless in its pursuit.

Bolan realized someone was panicking enough to set up the roadblock. They were desperate enough to step out in public in order to stop him.

What, he wondered, had Maggie Connor uncovered?

He eased off the gas, stepped on the brake and steadied the SUV as the tanker loomed larger. Armed figures stepped into view. There were three. One opened up with a submachine gun. Slugs scored the asphalt in front of the SUV. A second gunman started firing. Bolan saw sparks as bullets skidded off his hood. One hit the windshield, leaving a spiderweb crack. Bolan worked the wheel, the SUV rolling back and forth across the width of the road, tires squealing. A glance in the mirror showed the tail car maintaining a discreet distance now that the shooting had started. A small bonus.

The firing got heavier. One of the door mirrors exploded in a shower of plastic and glass.

Bolan stood on the brake, turning the wheel to bring the SUV around in a hard slide, broadside to the tanker. He thought for a moment that the vehicle might flip over. He switched off the ignition, cutting the power, pulled out his Beretta and, as the SUV came to a jarring stop, he slid across the seat and opened the passenger door. He rolled out and dropped to the road, crouching, before moving around the front of the vehicle.

Footsteps sounded nearby. Bolan picked up the first shooter as he moved into sight. The Beretta 93-R punched out a triburst that hit the man chest high and put him straight down. Maintaining his aggressive stance Bolan moved again, half rising as he cleared the front of the SUV and met the two remaining shooters head-on. His cool appearance, seemingly oblivious to the threat of the pair of armed figures, gave him a psychological advantage, and though it was only for a brief moment it was enough. Bolan triggered three-round bursts in a continuous volley, hitting both shooters before they acquired their target. They tumbled to the ground in agony, riddled by the 9 mm bursts.

The Executioner ran forward and snatched up one of the fallen weapons—an H&K MP-5. He checked the action and moved behind the SUV as the tail car fishtailed to a stop. An armed figure was leaning out the passenger door. Bolan raised the MP-5 and laid down a long, damaging burst that raked the front of the vehicle and blew the windshield out. The Executioner maintained his deadly fire, emptying the remainder of the magazine into the cab of the vehicle. When the MP-5 locked on an empty chamber he dropped it and returned to pick up one of the other discarded weapons.

There was no movement inside the tail car. As Bolan carefully checked it out he saw two bloody forms sprawled across the front seat. He turned back and crouched beside the other dead shooters. He removed the weapons he found. All five men were Hispanic. The only useful evidence he found was a cell phone on one of them. He dropped it in his pocket.

Bolan slid a fresh magazine into the Beretta, walked to the front of the tanker and climbed up to check the cab. He found a lone figure slumped behind the wheel. The rig's driver. Someone had put a couple of bullets in his body but he was still breathing. Bolan used the truck's radio to call for help. He located the first-aid box and did what he could to help the wounded trucker. Once he had the man settled as comfortably as he could Bolan used his own phone to call Hal Brognola.

"Sounds as if you've stirred somebody into action," the big Fed said.

"Panic more likely. Setting up an ambush in broad daylight on a public road says overreaction."

Brognola sighed. "What did Maggie stumble on to?"

"They didn't want me to get to Riba Bay. Maybe that's where I'll get some answers."

"Striker, I just got feedback from Bear. He has some results from the data you sent him. Riba Bay *is* your target." He read out an address. "Belongs to Raul Manolo, a suspected Colombian gunrunner. We're still analyzing the rest."

"Enough for me to go on," the Executioner said.

The wail of approaching sirens cut the air. Bolan saw vehicles in the distance.

"That the cavalry arriving?" Brognola asked.

"Yeah. I'll get back to you when I can."

As Bolan finished the call he saw a couple of Florida State Trooper cruisers rolling to a stop. Behind them was an ambulance. He stepped forward to meet the armed officers, showing his badge. A paramedic ran up behind the troopers.

"There's a man in the truck who needs medical attention," Bolan said. "He's been shot."

The medic nodded and waved his partner in. They

went directly to the rig. One of the troopers took a look around. He stared at the sprawled bodies.

"Damn," he said. "We'll be filling in forms for a week on this one. You want to tell me what the hell has been going on here, Agent Cooper?"

Colombia

The Executioner wasted no time. He couldn't be sure how far the sound of the shots might carry.

He turned to Ricco and unlaced the combat boots he was wearing. Then he loosened the belt holding the man's olive-green fatigues in place. Bolan stripped them off and pulled them over his own legs. He notched the belt tight around his waist. He sat down and pulled on the combat boots. They were near enough to his own size. He took his time with the laces, making sure the boots were secure before dragging the bloodied shirt from the body and pulling it on.

Crouching over Noriamo he freed the Uzi from around the dead man's neck, looping the cord over his right shoulder. He checked the body for extra ammunition and found a single clip in the man's back pocket. Stepping to where Santiago lay Bolan flipped open the blood-drenched linen jacket and saw the man had been carrying a 9 mm Beretta in a hip holster. The holster was held in place on Santiago's belt. Bolan freed the belt and slid the gun and holster off. He transferred it to his own belt. He took the Beretta out and checked the magazine. Full. He cocked the weapon and returned it to the holster.

He stood beside the cell door, breathing deeply as he looked at Maggie Connor.

He would not forget her.

And the men who had ordered her cruel death would not be forgotten.

Bolan opened the cell door and eased it back just enough to check the passage. It was deserted. At the far end a partially open door let bright sunlight pierce the gloom. That was his objective—reach the exit, then make another assessment. He slipped through the door, the Uzi ready in his hands. He broke from his stance and traversed the passage quickly. Flattened against the inner wall he peered out the open door.

He saw a rough-hewn compound, three crude huts. A stream ran across one side of the clearing. Dense green jungle pressed in on all sides. Bolan saw a flicker of movement to his right. An armed man in fatigues came into sight from behind one of the huts. He crossed the compound, lighting a thin cigar as he walked. An AK-74 dangled from a shoulder strap. The man looked relaxed. He was making his way in the direction of the cell block.

Bolan cleared the door, the Uzi up and spitting 9 mm slugs. He caught the approaching man before he had a chance to react. The guy twisted under the impact of the burst, dropping to his knees, then facedown. Bolan ran up close, snatching the AK from the guard's shoulder and looping the sling strap around his neck.

Bolan heard men calling out in Spanish. He pinpointed the location, bringing the Uzi back online so the armed figures piling out of one of the buildings at the sound of his first shots ran directly into the blazing volleys. Two figures tumbled to the ground, never really seeing the face of the man who had delivered them to quick death.

The others pulled back into the cover of the building they had just burst out of. Whatever they might have expected, the sight of the Executioner, in full killing mode, overwhelmed them. These gunmen were used to their victims being tied up and helpless without any will or skill to stand up to Raul Manolo's power.

By the time they pushed back outside, determined not to allow their prisoner to defy them, Bolan was out of their sights, his moving figure already fragmented and shadowy as he forged ahead into the surrounding jungle thicket.

Bolan's entry into the dense foliage was accompanied by the chatter of automatic weapons behind him. He heard the snap and whip of slugs penetrating the greenery, shredding leaves and thin branches. The moment he was swallowed and hidden temporarily from view he angled his line of travel. In the distance a number of voices called to one another, and more shots rattled from weapons.

The Executioner kept moving. The ground underfoot was soft and spongy, a layer of detritus from trees and bushes that had formed into a sound-deadening carpet over many years. The air was heavy and close, producing a cloying, sullen heat. Sweat began to form on Bolan's face and arms. He pushed on, maintaining as much speed as he could. He wanted to gain distance from his former captors. There was no way he was going back as a prisoner. If they were that desperate for his company they would pay a high price for it and for what they had already done.

As willing as his spirit was, Bolan's body began to reveal its weakened state after a few miles. Three days of brutal pounding had taken its toll. Mack Bolan was capable of strong actions but he was not invincible. Flesh and bone could absorb only so much before it began to rebel. He could feel his limbs growing heavier, his bruised ribs pulsing with pain. Keeping on the move was not the answer. Bolan knew he had to stand and fight, rather than lead his pursuers on a run that would drive him into the ground. He would have to make an educated guess as to the number of his enemies and deal with them on that basis.

He splashed over a stream, turned and crouched on his knees at the edge of the water. Behind him he could hear the distant sound of his pursuers. He knew they would pick up his trail eventually, so he worked quickly. He dropped his Uzi and reached down to scoop up soft mud from the edge of the stream. He smeared it liberally over his face and neck, ignoring the tender flesh. He coated arms and hands, then picked up the Uzi and retreated from the stream, turning to home in on the sounds made by the men following him.

He dropped back to wait, hidden among the dense foliage, blending in with his surroundings, waiting until he had a specific target. He would let his chosen man move well into range before he raised his weapon of choice.

The Beretta was set for single shots.

He could hear the guards working their way toward his general area, voices raised. They made no attempt to silence their approach as they made their way through the undergrowth. Bolan knew he wasn't dealing with seasoned jungle fighters. Urban streets were their normal haunts.

Okay, he thought, their loss, my gain.

The first target appeared, AK-74 cradled in the crook of one arm while he chattered on a com-set. Bolan watched him push through the greenery, his image flickering as he moved from one patch of light to another. The Executioner tracked him closely, waiting for his opportunity. He stroked the Beretta's trigger. The 9 mm slug hit the guard just above his left ear. He went down without a sound and before he hit the ground Bolan had pulled back, lost in the shadows again, his mud camouflage helping him to merge with his surroundings.

The sharp snap of the shot alerted the others. They froze, staring about them. Seeing nothing. Hearing nothing. The forest around them held shadows and light, and somewhere the man they were hunting. Com-sets buzzed with talk.

Bolan circled, picking out more wary figures. His enemies had no idea where he was now he had stopped running.

Target two was ahead of him. Less talkative than the others, he stood and listened to the jungle. His AK was up and ready as he sought *his* target. This guy was sharp. Alert. But it did him little good because the man he was looking for already had him in his sights.

Bolan fired a single fatal shot and the man went down.

He backed away from the killing ground and left the enemy unsure, searching and finding nothing but the dense forest.

He had counted three more, had observed their relative positions and allowed them to decide what they should do. Bolan was not in a forgiving mood. The people he had encountered since taking up his search for Maggie Connor were unrelenting in their savagery.

Not for the first time the thought entered his head that they were desperate to conceal something far bigger than illegal weapons. Ordnance, like drugs, was everyday trade to these people. The way they had responded to Maggie Connor's investigation supported the theory that it was on a higher level than narcotics and guns.

But what?

He had to extract himself from his current situation. While he was caught in this jungle, with a trio of unfriendly locals out for blood, he could do nothing at all.

Bolan picked up the tread of a boot to his immediate right. He curled his prone body and homed in on the slow-moving bulk of an armed man. Then he detected movement beyond the man in his line of sight. This one was twenty feet to the right. They were moving in tandem, covering a strip of the forest. They knew Bolan had gone to the offensive and were tracking with more care.

The second man stepped into a clearing. He was waiting for his partner to close in. Bolan braced himself. He saw the man turn, facing his way, presenting a wider target.

He held the image, eased back on the trigger, took his shot.

As the gunman went down Bolan swiveled and tracked his partner. He had reacted to the shot, aware it had come from only a short distance away from his own position. He swung his weapon around and began to pump shots into the foliage. Bolan felt the bullets chew at the greenery close by.

A slug skinned his right arm.

The Executioner held his position, watching the dark bulk of the shooter as he twisted to get a better look at his potential target.

It was a question of who would hit their target first.

Bolan's refusal to alter his own position allowed him that extra time to settle his aim and fire. He triggered a trio of shots, the Beretta hammering out its heavy sound in the closeness of the forest. The target flinched as the slugs hit him sidelong, angling up through his ribs to puncture lungs. He stumbled back with a heavy exhalation of breath before crashing solidly to the ground.

The Executioner picked up the merest flicker of sound behind him. Someone was really close.

The last man.

He caught a sliver of shadow on fronds to his left. The sliver expanded. Loomed over him. Instinct took over. Bolan rolled. He saw a dark shape towering over him, right arm already powering down, the intent to bury a machete deep into his skull. Bolan caught the blur of the blade as it slashed downward. Heard the soft *whoosh* as it cleaved the air. The blade pierced the ground as the Beretta fired. Bolan's attacker grunted as he caught the bullets in his torso. The man toppled and the machete remained buried in the soil, inches away from Bolan.

He pushed himself into a crouch and spent the next few minutes observing the forest around him. Apart from the constant bird chatter, he picked up no other sound. He spotted no further movement. Bolan stretched his wait for another ten minutes. He felt reasonably satisfied he was alone. For the moment. Sooner or later someone would contact the base. When they received no reply men would be dispatched to find out what was happening.

Bolan realized he was far from being in the clear.

5

The first drops of rain against his face woke the Executioner. He sat up, the Uzi on track until he realized what had alerted him. He could hear the heavy patter as the rain increased and became a downpour. Even with the cover of the forest he was soaked as he climbed to his feet. The water washed the camouflage mud from his face and arms. It had served its purpose.

Bolan took stock. Which way to go? Heading deeper into the jungle could be unwise. He might find himself in isolated territory. Miles from anywhere. He was poorly equipped. He had nothing to sustain himself. All he had were the weapons he was carrying. No food or water. No protective clothing. He wasn't even sure where he had been held.

Colombia?

Venezuela?

The background to Maggie Connor's investigation had mentioned both countries. Had he been brought to the border district by the subjects of Maggie's probing? His business in Florida had uncovered facts that pointed in that direction.

Bolan knew he wasn't going to find answers by standing around in the rain. He came to a decision. His only point of reference was the base he had escaped from. Back there he might find answers. He might also find transport out of the jungle. His captors had to have had some transport to get him to the place. A truck? Jeep? Or had they flown him in by helicopter? The thought registered and Bolan figured it the most likely. If so, the chopper would eventually return. He wanted to be there when it did.

He took his time retracing his steps. The steady pace kept his battered body from stiffening up while exercising his muscles. The rain stayed with him, hammering down with the ferocity only found in tropical climes. The already-soft jungle floor became waterlogged. The downpour soaked through to his skin. Despite the rain the temperature stayed warm, and once the downpour ended, the sullen heat would return with a vengeance. The enclosed atmosphere would trap the warmth in a steamy cocoon.

Bolan came to the edge of the jungle. He stared across the clearing at the silent base. There was no movement or sound. Just the bodies of the gunmen he had taken down on his exit from the cell block. He spent the next thirty minutes circling the area, viewing it from all angles and confirming his thoughts. The place was deserted and he saw no means of transport. On the farthest side of the clearing he spotted a flat patch that bore the imprint of a helicopter's landing gear. There were dark patches from oil seepage, as well.

He moved back to the cluster of buildings, still cautious.

There were three empty stone huts. One had an open frontage and served as a crude kitchen. There were sleeping quarters, with rough wooden pallets holding blankets. The final hut would have been the HQ and storage area. When Bolan went in he saw a radio transceiver against one wall. Equipment was strewn around the place. He spotted a case of bottled water. He opened one and took a long drink.

Crossing to the radio Bolan flicked on the power switch. The set remained dead. He followed a power cord and saw it disappear through the stone wall. He stepped outside and walked behind the building where a lean-to protected a portable generator unit. He checked out the small motor that drove the generator. About to fire it up he saw that someone had removed the lead that connected to the spark plug in the cylinder head. No spark, no ignition. No power to the radio. Someone had been thinking on his feet. The missing lead was probably in the pocket of one of the dead men back in the jungle.

The Executioner went to the makeshift kitchen and searched for food. In a metal locker he found some cans of corned beef. He broke the ring pull seal and opened a can. The smell of the meat made his empty stomach growl. He used his fingers to gouge out a portion and ate sparingly. He ignored the demands of his appetite. Overeating would be dangerous. He took the can with him as he returned to the HQ hut, and ate a little more corned beef, washing it down with some water. He moved one of the crude wooden chairs closer to the door to see the landing site. He ran a hand over his face, feeling the thick stubble that had grown during his captivity. He waited patiently, allowing his body to recharge.

THE DISTANT SOUND CAUGHT his attention. It rose and faded, broken up by the drumming of the rain on the roof. But it was a sound Bolan recognized instantly. Rotors beating the air.

The helicopter was getting closer. The sound was building. Then he saw it. A red, silver and blue Bell 206B3 JetRanger III. It came into sight above the tree line, angling down as it swooped over the base. Bolan watched it circle a number of times before the pilot settled it onto the landing site. The rotors began to slow as the power was cut. No one climbed out, even after the rotors ceased moving. They were being cautious. The guards had not shown themselves and radio silence remained.

The Executioner knew he would have reacted the same way given the circumstances.

Eventually, hatches opened and the pilot and his passenger climbed out. Both men were armed. Huddled together at the front of the chopper they discussed how to handle the situation. There was no doubt they had spotted the dead men.

Bolan ran a double check of his weapons. The reloaded Uzi was set to one side. He set an AK-74 for full auto mode. He knew the men were not there to ask after his welfare. He saw them move, AK assault rifles in their hands as they double-timed in the direction of the camp. They were aiming directly for the hut where Bolan was waiting.

He watched the two men as they closed in.

The lead man opened fire as he approached the hut. Bolan saw the wink of flame from the black muzzle.

He snapped up his own weapon, returning fire that ripped splinters from the door frame, then continued on to puncture the gunner's torso in a bloody spray. The man stumbled back, face contorted, mouth open in a warning shout. Bolan hit him with a second burst that rolled him along the side of the hut and dropped him facedown on the sodden ground.

A blur of movement showed in the open doorway. The second man ignored his partner's warning and ran directly into Bolan's line of fire. The Executioner held his finger on the trigger and cleared the magazine, blowing his target to shreds.

Crouching, he fed in a fresh magazine and cocked the assault rifle before he did anything else. He climbed to his feet, feeling the overwhelming fatigue returning, and knew if he didn't get some rest he was going to fall flat on his own face. He had to find out why he'd ended up at the camp and what Raul Manolo was planning. But first he had to make his final escape.

6

Florida

It was late by the time Bolan arrived in Riba Bay. He pulled in at the first motel he saw, took a room and slept through to morning. A long shower helped to clear his head. After a shave he dressed in fresh clothing, hung the shoulder rig under his jacket and walked to the diner across the road. He sat down and realized how hungry he was. The previous day had been too busy to allow him to eat. He ordered a solid breakfast and coffee.

While he waited he called Hal Brognola. The big Fed didn't sound too happy and grouched his way through the preliminaries.

"That set-to on the highway is going to take some time to settle. I didn't expect a small war to break out when I asked you to look for Maggie."

"Same goes for me." Bolan paused as the waitress brought his coffee. "Has Bear picked up anything else from her intel?"

"A couple of Cubans. Chico Delgado. Turns out he's a wheeler-dealer. And there's a government minister. Santos Perez."

"Mixed up with Colombians?"

"Struck me as curious."

"Anything on the crew who pulled the roadblock?"

"Bear pulled the rap sheets of the perps from the Florida State Trooper's database. Fingerprints identified three of them. They were all hard cases with records going back years. All had done time. One of them was linked with Raul Manolo a couple of years back."

"It's starting to look like Manolo doesn't want me treading on his toes."

"Striker, watch out for Manolo. His sheet reads like he's a career psycho. He's literally got away with murder on a number of occasions. It's like he's untouchable."

"Candidate for a visit, then," the Executioner said.

"Maggie made some mention of weapons trading. She hadn't pinned it down when her notes ran out."

"Colombian drug dealers. Cubans. Now guns. This is getting heavy."

"Yeah, tell me about it. I'm going to pass you over to Bear. He wants to download some images to your cell."

Kurtzman's gruff voice came through. "These were on the memory card from Maggie Connor's camera. They show some of the people she was watching, I guess. I've put names to the faces just to make it easy for you. Download coming through."

The waitress arrived with breakfast. Bolan placed the phone on the table while the download ran. His cell beeped as the download finished. He acknowledged the images and finished the call, then turned to his breakfast.

RAUL MANOLO STARED ACROSS the verandah at the ocean. With all that was going on, the last thing he had needed was the reckless act by his men. It had achieved nothing, except to alert the man named Cooper that he was under scrutiny. It had been bad enough when the search of the Connor woman's home revealed nothing. Whatever evidence she had gathered had not been hidden there.

The appearance of the man known as Cooper had been unexpected. His contact with Paul Sebring, though interrupted, had only proved that he was experienced. He had taken down the pair of interlopers with ease. The incident on the highway was another example of Cooper's skill. The road attack had been crude, ill-thought out and had resulted in total failure. The more Manolo heard about him, the stronger his desire to come face-to-face with the man.

What knowledge did Cooper possess? Had Maggie Connor passed along the information she had gathered? The retrieval of that information was vital, and if Cooper did know about it he had to be taken alive and interrogated.

Manolo smiled as he turned to his desk, sliding open a drawer and removing an automatic pistol. He placed it on the desktop, spinning it on the polished wood with a flick of his finger. He called his lieutenant and instructed him to keep Cooper under surveillance until ordered to take action.

Raul Manolo was a man with a mission.

THE EXECUTIONER LEFT the diner and walked along the street, away from the parked Jeep Cherokee he'd noticed circling the block earlier. He took his time, wanting to observe any reaction. Using store windows for their reflection he watched a figure step out of the vehicle and cross the street. The man stayed well back but he'd clearly taken the bait. Bolan saw a side street coming up, took the turn and continued walking. He maintained his relaxed pace, stopping occasionally to stare into store windows before moving on again. He gradually led the man away from the main drag.

Ahead of him Bolan saw the last of the stores give way to a mix of storage facilities and empty lots. He picked up his pace, as if he had spotted his ultimate destination, passing the first storage building, then making a turn that took him down the side of the facility. He spotted a stack of empty crates and slipped into a gap.

He heard footsteps on the loose gravel, followed by a muffled curse when the man realized his target had vanished. The footsteps moved faster as they headed in Bolan's direction. The man passed Bolan's hiding place, a gun in his hand.

The Executioner stepped out immediately behind his target. The touch of the Beretta's cold muzzle against the back of the man's neck brought him to a stop, hands raised in surrender. Bolan reached out and took away the handgun, transferring it to his own belt. He placed a hand on the guy's shoulder, turning him and pushing him against the closest stack of crates.

"You're making a mistake here, buddy."

"No mistake," Bolan said, "and I'm not your buddy. We don't even know each other."

The other man maintained his composure. "That's going to change when I show you something. Stay cool, I'm reaching into my back pocket."

He used his left hand to pull out a black leather object he raised above his head and flipped it open. Bolan glanced at it. He was looking at credentials that showed his man was ATF agent Brett Cassidy.

"Turn around," Bolan said.

When Cassidy about-faced he was confronted by Bolan's own badge. He scanned the information, shaking his head, a smile showing on his tanned face.

"Okay, Agent Cooper, we going to stand here all day flashing at each other? Or shall we swap stories?"

Bolan handed the man his gun and holstered his Beretta.

"Tell me yours and I'll tell you mine."

7

Colombia

The helicopter yielded useful information. Bolan found charts and radio frequency settings on a clipboard, along with course directions. Using them he worked out his location. He was fifty miles in from Valledupar, Colombia, and Valledupar had been one of Maggie Connor's last destinations, naming Raul Manolo's company, Santana, Inc., as a definite location. The Valledupar site was specified as a warehouse storage area.

Valledupar had a reputation as a tough town, where illegal dealing was the name of the game. If you wanted something and had the money to pay for it, Valledupar was the place to be. Goods were trafficked back and forth across the border, between Colombia and Venezuela. The region in and around the crossing was not one to be visited lightly. Death was one of the cheaper commodities and it took little arranging. The gangs who ran the border area were hard and had an uncompromising attitude toward anyone who showed up. Bolan didn't let the thought dissuade him. If his trail took him to Valledupar, so be it.

Bolan did things in order of priority.

He ate more of the corned beef he'd opened. He collected a number of the bottles of water and placed them inside the chopper. He also took a fully loaded Uzi and two AK-74 assault rifles with extra magazines.

With all that done the Executioner carried out his final task. He located a ground sheet and some webbing straps, and made his way back to the cell block. He pushed open the door of the interrogation room and crossed to the inner cell. Bolan laid the sheet down, then turned to Maggie Connor's suspended body. As gently as he could he removed it from the steel hook, laying her out on the ground sheet.

"Sorry we didn't reach you in time, Maggie," he said. "This isn't over yet."

Bolan wrapped her in the sheet, securing it with the webbing straps. He picked her up and carried her outside. He took her to the edge of the clearing and laid her down. He spent long minutes searching for stones to cover her. It was not the way he wanted to leave her, but there was little else he could do at the moment.

Finished, Bolan turned and walked away, heading for the waiting helicopter. He hardly noticed the rain had slackened. He climbed into the pilot's seat, closing the hatch behind him. Bolan studied the maps and flight notes. Satisfied he had his line of flight fixed in his mind he spent a few minutes familiarizing himself with the cockpit setup, before he started flicking switches. The still-warm engine caught on the first try. Bolan let the rotors turn and build up speed. As he felt the chopper start to move he increased the power, gently working the controls, and had the machine steady by the time it had reached tree level. Bolan turned the helicopter onto the correct heading and increased his forward speed. The base fell away behind him. The spread of the forest was all he could see ahead.

He was on course for Valledupar and answers to the questions crowding his mind.

He knew his appearance in Valledupar was not going to be welcomed. But that was fine. His intention was to spread fear and uncertainty throughout the organization responsible for Maggie Connor's death. They had a lot of blood on their hands, and the Executioner was certain that the deal they were working went far beyond simple gunrunning and drug peddling.

Someone in Valledupar knew the answers to his questions. One way or another he was going to find out.

IT WAS LATE AFTERNOON when Bolan saw Valledupar in the distance. He brought the chopper down on the first patch of clear earth he spotted, well outside the city limits. He cut the power, climbing into the passenger compartment behind the pilot's seat. He had spotted a bag of clothing on one of the rear seats and checked it out. He was able to get rid of the bloodstained shirt and replace it with a dark blue cotton one. He wore the shirt over the holstered Beretta. On the floor between the seats he found a grubby but serviceable baseball cap. With the peak pulled low he was able to conceal part of his battered, unshaven face. There was a worn canvas bag with a shoulder strap. Bolan found it would accommodate the Uzi and his spare magazine. He dropped in a couple of the bottles of water. He slid the other weapons under one of the seats, covering them with his abandoned shirt. Bolan had no choice over the helicopter. He was going to have to abandon it. If it was found and reported to the authorities there was little he could do.

Bolan struck out at a steady pace until he reached the road, then slowed, head down, shoulders hunched, making himself just another pedestrian.

Vehicles passed him, throwing up dusty clouds. Bolan ignored them. His mind was fixed on his ultimate destination. He wanted no contact with anyone else if it could be avoided.

As far as he was aware his enemies would not be looking for him yet. Once they realized they had lost contact with the jungle base and the helicopter crew, matters might change. When they found their missing chopper close to Valledupar, they would increase their efforts to find him.

It meant any window he had could be closed quickly if they suspected he was in their midst. So the Executioner wanted to make his presence known while he held the advantage.

He reached the city outskirts at dusk. Bolan made his way through the poorer sections where the inhabitants ran the daily course of their lives in quiet battles for food and work. As darkness fell and lights threw pools of illumination across the narrow, crowded streets, Bolan maintained his direct course. He could not avoid the crowds. Instead, he used them as cover, mingling with the ever-moving mass of humanity.

Bolan pressed on, a lone figure wandering the darkened byways of the city. But with a purpose unknown to anyone who might see him.

8

Florida

Brett Cassidy passed easily for a Florida native. He had lean good looks, a mop of fair hair and wore a bright shirt over light pants. Only the handgun and badge marked him as an ATF agent.

Bolan followed him from the alley to the man's parked Cherokee.

"I'm tracking a group we suspect are working up to a big arms deal," he said. "Right now I have Colombians out of Valledupar and a couple of Cubans. Somewhere in the mix I'm getting hints there may even be Americans involved." He paused, not wanting to voice too much.

"Looks as if we're working the same route," Bolan said. "Does the name Raul Manolo mean anything?"

Cassidy grinned. "He's why you're here? Manolo is one of the names on my list. I've been trying to tie him to this weapons deal. The guy is a heavy hitter in this part of the country. Tight connections from here to Valledupar. Knows people across the Caribbean. Runs a pretty mean crew."

"Yeah? I think I met some of them on my drive in yesterday," the Executioner said.

"No shit? That was *you?*" Cassidy's grin widened. "I

heard about that. Hell, Cooper, you will definitely not be on Manolo's guest list."

"I'm cut up knowing that. Does the name Maggie Connor mean anything to you?"

Cassidy shook his head. "No. Is she part of your team?"

"Part of my investigation."

"Is she involved with Manolo?"

"Only in a peripheral way." Bolan checked the street again. "You got a team around you?"

"No. I'm working solo. This is a busy town. Manolo has too many eyes and ears in his employ. Dragging a damn posse along with me would be like waving a flag. I work on my own. Same as you."

Interesting, Bolan thought. He let the comment pass, simply storing it for future reference.

"You got plans?" Cassidy asked casually.

Bolan shook his head. "After what happened I'm walking light. Need to hang around and watch the world go by until I get clearance from base. You know the way it goes. Spend the biggest percentage of operations time waiting for orders. That little run-in on the road has made them reconsider how we need to handle this. So I'm going to check out the beach and count bikinis."

Cassidy nodded. "Hell of a way to earn a living, huh? I have to get back to Miami. The suits have called a case meeting." He turned to go. "Hey, maybe we'll see each other again, Cooper."

Bolan nodded. "Maybe we will."

SOFT WARM DARKNESS cloaked the Executioner. The shadows offered cover, aiding his silent movements, drawing in around him like old friends.

Raul Manolo's sprawling villa overlooked the curve of Riba Bay. Soft music floated out across the lush estate.

Bolan was already inside the compound, crouching in concealment at the base of the perimeter wall, thick foliage surrounding him. He could make out maybe a half dozen figures around the large swimming pool. Lights from the house spilled out across the tiled terrace. It was a low-key gathering. No female company. There looked to be several earnest discussions taking place. A business meeting, perhaps. Bolan had to wonder what kind of business.

Glancing at his watch he saw it was 8:36 p.m. Early yet. Time for other guests to arrive. He could only watch and wait. Intel gathering was time-consuming, with no guarantee it would produce anything of value. He settled with his back against the trunk of a curving palm. He had the capacity to wait it out as long as it took. He would simply remain in concealment and allow the enemy to come to him.

Forty minutes later Bolan's interest peaked when more people walked out from the house and joined the group around the pool. There were three men—one principal, the other two his minders. It showed in the way they flanked the man, never relaxing, even though they were on safe ground. The lead man crossed to confront the man Bolan had already identified as Manolo. They shook hands, Manolo gesturing to his guest to sit in the empty lounge next to his own. Drinks were poured. The newcomer removed his suit jacket, took his glass and bent in close to Manolo. They began an intense discussion.

Soft sounds suddenly alerted Bolan. He eyeballed an

armed guard in light clothing moving around the grounds. The man wore a slender headset, with a thin microphone. He passed within a couple of feet of the Executioner, unaware he was under close scrutiny. The security man moved on, continuing his wide sweep of the property, the house always in his sights.

Attention back on the pool group, Bolan sensed they were there for the duration. Others had joined in the discussion. It was animated but not heated. He figured this was his best opportunity to get inside the house.

He crouched low, using the shadows and the heavy shrubs as cover, working his way closer to the house. Along the side of the structure, away from the illuminated pool area, the shadows were deeper and he reached the base of the exterior wall with no challenges. He made his way to the opening that allowed access to an interior courtyard. Bolan eased over the low wall, crouching at its base to scan the area. He saw carefully tended flower beds, a carved stone fountain trickling water into a wide base. Concealed lights bathed the courtyard in soft illumination.

The courtyard was quiet. So much so that the soft tread of the armed guard reached Bolan's ears again, alerting him to the man's presence. The guy moved into a patch of light, pausing as he spoke into his headset in Spanish. The man signed off, completing his circuit of the courtyard before moving away.

Bolan pushed to his feet and turned to the right, heading in the opposite direction to the guard. A tiled walkway led from the courtyard to an open door and the main house. He unleathered the Beretta and flicked the selector to single shot. He eased through the doorway into a tiled passage that led to a large living area. The hallway had a door on Bolan's right. It opened to his touch and he peered inside. It was a book-lined library and office. His interest was drawn to the large desk where the flat-screen monitor for a computer showed light. He stepped inside and crossed to view the screen, tucking his Beretta back into its shoulder holster. The monitor showed a generic screen saver. Leaning over the desk Bolan hit the space bar and the image vanished. He was faced with a text screen containing two words in Spanish.

Paso Trasero.

Bolan worked the words around in his mind until the translation came.

Back Step.

He scrolled down the screen to go to the next page, but the only thing that showed was a password bar.

He checked out the rest of the desk, opening drawers and going through the contents. The only interesting items were a couple of checkbooks—one in the name of Raul Manolo, the second for a company called Santana, Inc. He flipped open the book and removed the last check, folding it away in one of his blacksuit pockets. He returned both checkbooks to their original places and closed the drawer.

Straightening, Bolan took a long look around the room. Nothing else struck a chord suggesting he inspect it more closely. He was about to move when he heard the sound of someone approaching the room.

The Executioner had assessed the entrance and exit possibilities before he had stepped inside. Apart from the door the only other way out was through the windows.

The windows were on the side of the house he had entered via the courtyard. They were his only option.

The door swung open, revealing an armed figure, muzzle of his handgun sweeping the room. Bolan saw it pause, settling on his dark outline. He reacted instantly, turning and dropping to a crouch. He heard the crack of the weapon, even picked up the thud of the slug coring into something solid. Then he was moving, using the heavy desk as cover. The distant windows were his objective.

Behind him he heard a muttered curse, then the second shot. The slug bit into the padded upright of an armchair, inches above Bolan's head. He shoulder rolled, pulled his legs under him and powered himself forward. The shooter anticipated the move. The Executioner launched himself in a full-length dive toward the closest window. The shooter fired again, and in the instant before Bolan hit the window frame, he felt the stinging bite of the slug as it seared across the top of his left shoulder. Then he was surrounded by splintered wood and a glittering shower of shattered glass, his body arching out and down. His outstretched hands made contact with the grass, his forward momentum carrying him into a long roll, body absorbing the shock of landing. Bolan twisted over on his side, drawing his legs under him to push upright, clawing the Beretta from its holster. He was on the right course for his exit point.

A harsh yell split the night air. He heard the sound of another shot. Bolan didn't break his stride. His only course was forward, to the wall and over. He didn't look back. Couldn't see what had happened to the group around the pool. His sole objective was to get out and away before Manolo's security team could get themselves organized.

Bolan closed in on the heavy shrubbery ahead. Suddenly a figure broke from the greenery, moving quickly, submachine gun cradled in his arms and rising as he stepped into Bolan's path. It was the first guard he had seen on his initial entry. Increasing his speed, the Executioner hit the man head-on, his right shoulder driving into the guard's chest. The all-out impact pushed the breath from the man's lungs. He grunted once as he was propelled backward. He crashed against the trunk of a palm tree, his gun's barrel jerking skyward and his finger tripping the trigger. The short crackle of automatic fire was loud in the comparative quiet. Bolan reached out with his left hand, palm spread over the guard's face. He slammed the man's head back, his skull crunching against the hard tree trunk. The guard dropped instantly.

A second automatic weapon opened up from behind Bolan. A burst of bullets splintered the tree trunk. The Executioner turned, stepping behind the tree for cover, bringing up the Beretta. He spotted a guard running in his direction. Bolan raised the Beretta and triggered a pair of 9 mm shots. The guard stumbled, missed his footing and went down on his knees. He dropped his weapon and clutched at his side, where blood was already pouring from the wound. Bolan turned away, catching a brief glimpse of figures milling around the pool.

Whatever else he might have done, his visit had certainly broken up the party.

He pulled back into the deeper shadows, moving without pause as he retraced his steps and hauled himself up and over the wall. It wasn't his most elegant retreat from a probe, but at least he'd come away with something.

Santana, Inc.

It was simply a name on a check. But it was something he could run by Aaron Kurtzman. The Stony Man computer wizard could work his magic and make the name speak to him.

Bolan jogged back to where he had concealed his SUV a quarter mile down the approach road. He unlocked the vehicle and pulled a leather jacket over the holstered Beretta. He could feel the sharp pulse of pain from where the bullet had torn across his shoulder. He ignored it. It would wait until he got back to the motel.

He kept an eye on his rearview mirror as he drove. He turned the SUV around and put it on the road back to town, watching for signs of any pursuit. The road was quiet and Bolan got the feeling that Manolo wasn't going to initiate any kind of mass chase. Whatever the man was into Bolan guessed he wanted it to remain low-key. Any kind of overt action issuing from his estate could involve interest from the police. Bolan was sure the man would fume and rant, but if he did anything it would be done discreetly.

Somewhere along the way Manolo and Bolan were going to lock horns.

It was bound to happen.

MANOLO WAS CLOSE TO exploding with rage, yet he managed to contain his anger. He led the way into the house, to the library, where he surveyed the damage.

"He came into my house," he said, the emotion in his

voice letting everyone know how he felt. "He came into my house. I will make him regret that to the moment he dies. No one enters my house without my permission." Manolo took a long breath, forcing his emotions down.

He walked around his desk and stared at the monitor screen.

Paso Trasero.

"He has seen this?" he shouted.

"He was in here. Likely he did. It won't mean anything to him," someone said. "Just words on a screen. Meaningless on their own."

Manolo considered that. "Let us hope so. I think it is time we did something about this man Cooper. He is beginning to annoy me. I have to leave for Colombia later tomorrow. We will arrange for Agent Cooper to accompany us. As he seems interested in my property he can spend some time with Santiago at our place in the country."

Everyone knew what he meant. It drew a subdued ripple of laughter from the assembled group.

"Agent Cooper. *Mi casa es su casa.*"

9

Colombia

It was close to five in the morning and the Executioner had his target in sight.

The building was gray in the emerging dawn. Only a few lights showing. The compound looked deserted. The sprawling site was surrounded by a wire fence, entry via a metal gate with a wooden security hut. It was far from what Bolan considered high-concept, high-security. He reminded himself he was in Colombia, where men of Raul Manolo's stature were all-powerful.

In Valledupar, Manolo would consider it a sign of weakness to cower behind electric fences. From what Bolan had learned of the Santana, Inc., operation it was low on Manolo's pecking order. The company handled small-time consumables up-front. Behind the scenes were the more profitable items, kept separate from the man's main business at his other bases. Santana, Inc., based on Maggie Connor's research, was where Manolo ran his gunrunning operation.

And gunrunning was linked to Back Step.

Bolan did a final weapons check. He was as ready as he was going to be. He eased out from cover and negotiated his way down the dusty slope overlooking the site.

Minutes later he was studying the security hut, seeing the heavyweight guard lolling back in his seat, a half-smoked cigar hanging from his right hand. The man was immersed in a magazine. Bolan circled the hut and followed the line of the fence. As he made his silent foray Bolan checked for more security personnel. In the ten minutes he spent, he saw no sign of any movement. That did not signify anything definite. There might be others deeper within the site. If Manolo had weapons awaiting dispatch any security would be centered around them.

Pushing his way through a tangle of heavy brush Bolan saw a sagging section of fence that would allow him to penetrate the site. He eased aside the loose links and slipped through. The area had an untidy look about it. He saw stacks of barrels. And empty packing cases. A number of forklift trucks sat parked where their operators simply left them at the end of a work shift.

Bolan used the detritus of the place to provide his cover as he worked his way to the main warehouse. There were a number of security lights on metal poles, but their wide spacing meant plenty of dark patches to offer him cover. He reached the first storage warehouse and listened for any sounds of activity. Nothing. He moved on, deeper into the site. It was not until the third building that he picked up sound.

The main door had been pushed back on its rollers. Peering around the edge Bolan saw armed men loading boxes into a long panel truck. Bolan had seen the box configurations enough to be able to recognize them. They were ordnance cases. The size and shape suggested automatic rifles. The boxes were being removed from a wooden loading pallet.

Someone called out to him.

The shouted challenge came from behind Bolan.

He dropped, swiveling at the hip, the Uzi rising. Bolan recognized the guard from the security hut. He had roused from his early morning reading with a vengeance, now wielding a heavy pump-action shotgun that he raised and fired in Bolan's direction. His shot was close but not close enough. At the range he was shooting, the power of the guard's shotgun blast was severely restricted and the spread took away the lethal impact of the burst. Bolan heard pellets rattle against the warehouse door at shoulder height, stray remnants tugging at his sleeve. He swept the advancing guard with a savage burst from the Uzi that cut the guy off at the knees. The guard uttered a scream of agony as his lower limbs were suddenly bloodied and mashed. Falling, his weapon spilling from his fingers, he descended into his own private hell.

Bolan turned, seeing the loading crew start to scatter. One of the boxes was dropped as hands went for weapons. As the box hit the floor it burst open, spilling gleaming rifles onto the concrete.

Moving inside the warehouse, hugging the inner wall, Bolan sprayed a burst from the Uzi, hitting the closest of the loading crew. The man pitched facedown on the floor, his weapon skidding across the concrete. The sight of one of their own going down galvanized the others into action, and the Executioner moved position along the front of the warehouse, hugging the wall where the shadows were deepest. He heard the whine and slap of automatic fire. He rolled behind a pile of crates.

He had made a swift count of the opposition. With one down that left five. All were armed and with a better knowledge of the warehouse layout than Bolan.

One of the crew decided to make his own move, suddenly breaking away from the main group. He cut off at an angle, firing as he did. His shots were wide of any mark, delivered in an attempt to force Bolan to remain undercover. His strategy might have worked if he had thought it through. Bolan heard the slugs slam into the wood crates a few feet away as the man fired on the run. He tracked in with the Uzi and hit the moving target with a short burst that spun him sideways. The man stumbled, falling to one knee, shocked by the impact of the 9 mm slugs. Bolan did not allow him time to recover. He raised the muzzle of the Uzi and planted a second burst that hit chest high, putting down the target permanently.

A brief lull in the enemy fire gave Bolan the opportunity to move yet again, crouching as he made it to the end of the stack of crates. Rounding the final one, he emerged behind the loading crew, and set up a stunning volley from the Uzi that hit hard and fast. The crew were caught unprepared and before any of them were able to re-position Bolan mowed them all down. As the final man dropped, the Executioner reached into his bag and took out the fresh Uzi magazine. He made the exchange swiftly without taking his eyes off his targets. Not that it mattered. His deadly bursts had been fatal.

He moved among the downed crew's bodies, removing every weapon he found and throwing them inside the open rear of the panel truck. Aware that he might be running out of time Bolan checked the boxes already inside. Among the mix of crates were some that bore U.S. military markings. Inside the boxes were American M4s and loaded magazines. He found some Beretta 92-Fs. He also found U.S. military uniform sets, boots and accessories. Checking the main consignment Bolan located a couple of cases of explosive compound. In a separate pack he found timed fuses. Breaking open one of the explosive compound packs Bolan set one in the van itself. He placed another on the boxes on the warehouse floor. He took timers, setting them in position with the explosives, and activated them. He allowed five minutes before detonation.

Retracing his steps Bolan exited the warehouse and faded into the darkness, heading for the gap in the perimeter fence where he had gained entry. Deep in the covering shadows of dense shrubs he waited. In the early morning stillness the explosion was deafening, the glare of the detonation intense. The front of the warehouse disintegrated, debris hurled in every direction. The crackle of exploding ammunition sounded like a string of firecrackers. The flames rose in the predawn sky as the timber construction of the warehouse ignited. Smoke hung in the still air as Mack Bolan slipped away.

NO ONE SPOKE. They stood around in nervous silence as Raul Manolo made his inspection of the burned wrecks of the panel truck and warehouse. They gazed at the blackened, twisted remains of the weapons and the charred, heat-shriveled bodies of the loading crew.

Manolo himself had barely spoken since his arrival. He was tight-lipped during his inspection of the destruction. Finally he walked from the warehouse and crossed to his waiting limousine, his people following at a discreet distance.

"Dega."

The man hurried to Manolo's side.

"Are we certain it was the American?"

"Escobar was on the gate. He challenged the man before he was shot. I spoke to him before he was taken to the hospital. His description fits the man Cooper. We know he escaped and took our helicopter and abandoned it on the far side of the city."

"And yet we still do not know how much the bitch Connor told him. Dega, we need to find him. Put on as many men as you can to locate him. He's one man. An American. Flood the streets. I'll pay a bounty to whoever finds him. Get everyone we have on our books." When Dega did not move as quickly as expected Manolo raised his voice for the first time that morning. "Do it now!" he screamed.

Dega hurried away, shouting orders to the waiting crew members.

Inside the limousine Manolo picked up the phone and tapped in a speed-dial number. He spoke the moment it was picked up.

"There has been an incident. I need you to duplicate my order as soon as possible. Most important is the special package you obtained. That is priority. The American military merchandise. Yes, I understand it is not as simple as taking goods from a supermarket shelf. I know there will be additional costs. I expected that, and as I told you before, money is not a problem. Be advised that we have someone interfering with our operation. I thought it only courteous to alert you to this in case he reached out as far as you. We know him only as Cooper. Some kind of operative from your Justice Department. Why he is involved is incidental. Just be warned. Contact me the moment you have the goods arranged."

Manolo put down the phone. He instructed his driver to leave the site. The American, Cooper, had become a major problem. His escape from Santiago's confinement and the elimination of the interrogation crew showed that the man had considerable skills. His visit to Santana, Inc., and the destruction of the weapons, had turned out to be unfortunate. But not fatal to the upcoming operation. The timing was bad, yes. But it would not wreck the plan.

Paso Trasero would go ahead as scheduled.

Nothing could stop it now.

10

Florida

In his motel room Bolan stripped and got under the shower. The warm water stung the bullet wound on his shoulder, making him gasp. He soaped the tender spot and saw blood splash at his feet. Out of the shower he dried off, wrapped a towel around his waist and returned to the room. He took a white T-shirt from his bag, wadded it and held it over the wound on his shoulder. Sitting on the edge of his bed he used his cell phone to make contact with Stony Man Farm. He gave Brognola a quick summary of the night's exercise, then asked for Kurtzman.

"See what more you can find out about Santana, Inc. I'm looking at a check from a bank in the Cayman Islands." Bolan read off the account details. "Took it from Manolo's desk. Be interesting to see what it brings up. I also picked up a name from his computer. In Spanish. *Paso Trasero*. Means Back Step. Couldn't get anything more."

"I'll do what I can. I managed to pull some more details from Maggie Connor's memory chip. Ran the images through various databases and came up with some interesting stuff. Manolo has an operation on the Colombia–Venezuela border. Along with Chico

Delgado and assorted unsavory characters. Maggie caught the guy in Valledupar. Street café. Raul Manolo, Chico Delgado and an American named Douglas Kirby. I ran his picture through U.S. military databases. The guy is U.S. Army. Rank of major. I pulled his service details. He's coming to the end of his last tour. Guy's not exceptional, so he's never been promoted any higher. Looks like he's been treading water for a number of years. No family. No ties outside the military. Maybe he's looking to bulk up his pension with some extracurricular deals?" Kurtzman said.

"What's his specialty?"

Kurtzman gave a short laugh. "Take a guess, Striker. Hell, I'll tell you, anyway. Weapons supply. He's an ordnance guy."

"We're picking up signals here," Bolan said. "Right now I haven't got them in the correct order."

The Executioner ran through the names he had and their origins.

Cubans, Colombians. And an American military man.

What had brought them together?

With a need for weapons, too.

Maggie Connor appeared to have uncovered some can of worms. It just needed untangling.

Bolan let the permutations have free rein while he used the small first-aid kit from his bag and placed a dressing over his shoulder wound.

Dressed in civilian clothing, the shoulder-holstered Beretta under his jacket, he took a walk to a nearby restaurant and ordered a light meal and coffee. He was partway through his main course when his phone rang. It was Barbara Price, Stony Man Farm's mission controller.

"Hey, Striker. Update time."

"I'm all ears."

"Santana, Inc., has holdings in the U.S., corporate HQ in Miami. They have a warehousing facility near the water, as well. There's also a distribution site in Valledupar, Colombia, and others in and around the Caribbean. Smaller units in Panama. The checking account *is* with a Cayman Island bank, so no surprise there. Manolo does a lot of offshore dealing. All kinds of agency detail the Bear managed to dredge up. Manolo is suspected of nefarious dealings but the guy has a hell of a legal team backing him. Friends in high places, as well. Remind me, how many times have we had this conversation with each other?"

"It's the nature of the beast," Bolan reminded her.

"Any more thoughts on Maggie Connor?" Price asked.

"Plenty of thoughts. None of them encouraging."

"Along the lines she might have been silenced?"

Bolan's pause gave Price her answer.

"The way her staff were dealt with showed how these people work. If they believe she gathered information that might expose them I don't think they would hesitate to kill her."

"Did anything come through on Brett Cassidy, our friendly ATF man?"

"Six years with the department. Prefers to work solo, if he can. Reasonable record. Aaron is checking into his personal details and finances."

"He looks clean?"

"For now, maybe."

"But?"

"But what? Did I say *but?*"

"Uh-uh. I'll stay sharp."

"Damn right you will, Striker."

"Talk later."

Bolan ended the connection. He digested the brief conversation with Price. Her unspoken feelings over Cassidy matched his own misgivings about the ATF agent. Since his earlier meeting with the man a faint, persistent thread of caution had been nibbling away at him. What was it about Cassidy that wouldn't settle? That chance remark about Bolan working as a loner? Had Cassidy seen something of himself in Bolan? An off-the-cuff remark that went no further? Or a slip showing Cassidy knew more about Bolan than he should?

Bolan finished his meal, paid the tab and walked back to his motel. He unlocked the door and stepped into the dark room. He recognized the sweet aroma instantly. The first time he had registered it had been in Maggie Connor's home. The crushed butt of a cigar left by one of the killers who had slaughtered the house staff.

He slid his hand under his jacket, fingers brushing the butt of the Beretta.

It was as far as he got.

He sensed movement to his right. Something hard struck across the side of his head. The Executioner fell back against the wall as the room's shadows seemed to converge on him. He knew there were more of them.

Hands grabbed his arms and swung him around. A hard fist slammed into his mouth, the blow tearing his lip. Bolan fought back, kicking out, and heard a man curse in Spanish. His action brought a rain of blows.

"His jacket. Get the fucking jacket off," someone said in English.

Pale light shone from the bedside lamp as it was switched on. Enough to outline the figures encircling Bolan. He continued his struggle, but overwhelming numbers held him firmly.

Hands gripped Bolan, pushing him down, pinning him in the angle where the wall met the floor. The figures surrounded the Executioner, subduing him.

Then he saw the hand descend, holding a hypodermic syringe, the needle glistening. The hand dipped. Bolan felt the sharp sting as the needle penetrated his left arm. He felt the effects within seconds. A warm, comforting glow started to spread through his body. His struggles weakened and despite his inner strength the drug won out.

His final clear image before it all broke up was of a man in the back of the room who moved out of the shadows and briefly into Bolan's line of vision, unaware that Bolan had not fully lapsed into unconsciousness.

Brett Cassidy.

11

Colombia

Daylight came swiftly. Bolan distanced himself from the destruction, heading to the main highway and toward the border with Venezuela. He started to look out for some kind of transport.

It was going to make it harder for him to stay concealed. But Manolo's search teams would be out looking for him. Bolan knew that as a fact.

Kidnapping Bolan and taking him to Colombia had been a deliberate act. Brought about because of what Manolo *suspected* Bolan knew. It smacked of desperation. There was an operation in the planning stage. Something that was going to happen shortly and Manolo was involved. If facts concerning that operation were leaked it would have to be cancelled. It didn't take a genius to work that out. Hence, the lengths Raul Manolo was prepared to go to keep those facts concealed.

The Executioner had few facts. He had no idea what was behind Manolo's actions, just that the man was running scared. He had to find out what Manolo was involved in. To do that he needed to stay free.

There were few road signs for Bolan to follow. His knowledge of the area was nonexistent, so he trusted his instincts and his sense of direction. The scant information from the signs he did spot told him he was moving in the right direction. The border crossing into Venezuela held the best promise for his chance to reach some kind of safe haven.

Traffic was light. What vehicles he did see were strictly local. Produce trucks. The odd ramshackle car swaying by on uncertain suspension. Bolan avoided any contact. He couldn't be certain how trustworthy anyone could be. And he was reluctant to involve any locals in case they found themselves caught up in a threatening situation if Manolo's men showed up on the scene.

When he spotted a late-model Toyota SUV cruising the dusty back road Bolan was instantly alert. The vehicle looked entirely out of place in this isolated backwater. He maintained his pace. Head down, shoulders hunched in the subservient attitude of a lowly peasant who had no thoughts of anything except going on his way.

The SUV drew level with Bolan. The Executioner kept moving, outwardly paying no attention to the expensive, dusty vehicle. Beneath the lowered peak of his cap Bolan's eyes picked up the bulk of the SUV as it stopped beside him. He saw the passenger window slide down. A hard-faced man stared at him, cold eyes raking the shabbily dressed form. Bolan spotted the tip of a gun muzzle resting against the window frame.

The observer said something to one of his companions. He turned back to Bolan, the door clicking open. The man stepped out of the SUV, hands out of sight behind his back.

"Hey, come here."

The call was delivered in English. A deliberate challenge. Bolan ignored it.

Then the order came in Spanish and Bolan had to respond. He stopped walking and turned slowly, still maintaining his deferential pose.

"Show me your face, lazy one," the man said in Spanish.

Bolan raised his head, holding the man's gaze.

From inside the SUV someone spoke, leaning across to get a better look.

"...could be him. The American. Cooper..."

Bolan saw the rigid set in the man's shoulders as mind and eye made recognition. Then he was turning his upper body back in Bolan's direction, right hand starting to sweep around, the blurred shape of a pistol in his fist.

The Executioner dropped to a semicrouch, his hand sweeping aside his loose shirt, fingers closing over the butt of the holstered Beretta. He drew, thumbing off the safety, pushing the muzzle at his target. Bolan triggered two close-spaced shots, putting both 9 mm slugs into the man's chest, then angled the pistol at the open window. He triggered three fast shots into the SUV, heard a groan and the blowout of window glass on the opposite side of the SUV. He was aware of movement behind dark glass in the rear of the vehicle, the door starting to open. As he powered along the length of the SUV, Bolan triggered more shots through the widening gap of the rear door. A startled grunt followed, the door bursting open as a body fell free. The man hit the road hard, his own weapon spilling from his fingers as he struck the dusty surface.

At the rear of the SUV, Bolan was briefly out of sight

of the enemy. He dropped the Beretta and pulled open the bag around his neck, grabbing the Uzi and bringing it online. He saw the dark outline of someone emerging from the far side of the vehicle, the guy yelling in wild Spanish that did little except pinpoint him. He came barreling around the end of the SUV, directly into the spitting fire of the Uzi. The 9 mm slugs caught him waist high, then climbed as Bolan raised the muzzle. His steady burst struck hard, spinning the guy along the side of the SUV before dumping him facedown on the unyielding road. Bolan straightened up, tracked in on the SUV's rear window and put a long burst through the glass into the passenger compartment.

Fragments of glass rattled as they fell inside the SUV. A haze of dust drifted. Inside the vehicle a man groaned, the SUV rocking slightly as a heavy body slumped. Bolan picked up a subdued sound that he realized was the still-running motor. He circled the SUV, the Uzi leveled on the vehicle, watching for signs of life. He paused beside the open passenger door. The driver had fallen across the seats, bloody and motionless.

He opened the rear door and checked inside. One more hard man sprawled inelegantly in the foot well. Blood had spattered the seats from the wounds opened by the Uzi.

Bolan backed away. Whatever else he might be Raul Manolo was thorough. It proved to the Executioner that his escape route to the border was going to be well covered. Manolo had figured correctly that he would be smart enough to stay to the back roads, avoiding the main highway.

Bolan reloaded the Uzi with a fresh magazine. He

picked up the Beretta, dropping it back in the holster. He picked up the sound of approaching vehicles. They were coming in fast, from both directions along the road. They were too quick for him to outrun. They swooped in, blocking his escape and were still sliding to a stop when armed men emerged, enough of them to fan out and cover Bolan from all sides.

This time, it appeared, there was nowhere for him to run.

The Executioner knew when to fight and when to submit. Right now there were too many of them to take on. Bolan lowered the Uzi, watching and waiting.

The men surrounding him made no overt moves. They simply stood and waited.

A tall, broad figure stepped out from one of the cars and walked through the waiting group. He was a powerful figure. Black hair was just starting to show a few gray flecks. A thick mustache covered his upper lip. His impassive face was turned in Bolan's direction. Dark eyes fixed on the American. Unblinking, holding Bolan's own steady gaze. The man stopped a few feet away, head turning to take in the scene. Observing the bullet-riddled SUV and the bodies of Manolo's hit squad he returned his gaze to Bolan.

"Agent Cooper, put down the gun. We need to talk. But not here."

12

"Hand over your weapons," the man instructed. "It will serve us both best if you do."

While the Executioner considered his options the man turned and gave rapid instructions in Spanish to his men. Most of them moved toward the SUV and the bodies. However, one of them remained with the leader, his gun still trained on Bolan.

"Your weapons. Please."

The man was facing Bolan again, holding out his hand. Stepping forward Bolan handed him the Uzi, then passed over the Beretta. The man took them and gave a slight nod.

"Come with me."

Bolan turned and followed the man to one of the cars. They climbed into the backseat. The gunman slid in beside the driver. Nothing else was said as the car swung around and picked up speed. The man who had extended the invitation turned in Bolan's direction and handed the Beretta back to him. Somewhat surprised, Bolan took the weapon and slid it into the holster beneath his shirt. He saw the gesture as a peace offering. A way of telling him he was not in the presence of his enemy. He sat back, wondering what would happen next.

The car was moving quickly. The driver was plainly

familiar with the area as he wound back and forth along narrow back roads. Eventually they emerged on an approach road to a low-rise villa-type house overlooking a curving valley. The heavy wooden gates swung open automatically and they drove onto the walled property. They followed a hard-packed driveway and came to a stop alongside the front entrance.

Bolan had not missed the armed men patrolling the grounds.

The man beside Bolan leaned forward.

"You are quite safe here, Agent Cooper," he said as he got out of the car.

Bolan stepped out and took a long look around, his mind storing what he saw.

"I really do not think you will need to use an emergency route," the man said as he watched.

"Habit," Bolan said.

"I understand your caution and I respect it. But I assure you there is no danger here."

Bolan was led inside the villa. It was cool and quiet, the interior furnished tastefully.

"Take a seat. I will hazard a guess that you have not eaten properly for some time?"

"I've had other things on my mind," Bolan said.

"We will change that for you."

"I could go for a cup of coffee," Bolan admitted.

His host nodded and ordered one of his men to prepare some food.

"Time for introductions, I believe. I am Commander José Calberon. I am in charge of this unit. We are a task force set up via the Colombian Ministry of Justice, under a direct order of the president himself.

We are directed to target criminal groups and do whatever it takes to eradicate them. We have no restraints, report to no one, and I make all command decisions. Very few people know of our existence. It seems, Agent Cooper, you have strayed directly into the line of fire. Our current target is Raul Manolo and his organization."

"Any straying has been forced on me by the man himself."

Calberon took an armchair facing Bolan. He waited until coffee arrived in a large insulated jug and was placed on a low table between them. He poured mugs for each of them.

"What is your interest in Manolo?" Calberon asked.

The Executioner explained what he knew about Raul Manolo and his group. He described what had taken place in Florida and how he had ended up in Manolo's jungle compound.

"This unfortunate woman had stumbled on to something Manolo is planning, you say?"

"Her information pointed in that direction, but Maggie Connor's data only hinted at some kind of conspiracy."

"But her investigation frightened Manolo into serious actions," Calberon said. "That suggests to me there has to be something larger going on."

"Your own investigations haven't noticed anything unusual?" Bolan asked.

"No. Perhaps because all we have been concentrating on are his regular activities. Drugs. Illegal trading back and forth across the border with Venezuela. You are, I suppose, aware of the dealing that goes on in this area?"

"Yes."

"We do have our own intelligence sources. Individuals who look and listen for us. That is how we became aware of your presence here in Valledupar and of Manolo's frantic search for you. We had been searching for you ourselves and picked up information about one of Manolo's squads in the area. I apologize for our slow response. The back roads where we located you are extremely isolated. However, it seems you handled the situation credibly on your own."

"At least you did show up," Bolan said. "Local information must be hard to get around here."

"There are times when we get nothing. I have a couple of covert members of my team on the streets, posing as drug dealers. Unfortunately Manolo also has his sources and I frankly admit his network is probably more successful than ours. He can afford to pay better. And his reputation works for him. Anyone who offers us information demands to be protected. Manolo's reprisals are savage. In our country, Agent Cooper, the power and influence of the criminals far outstrips anything we can offer. They get stronger, have more influence, work their way into government departments." Calberon smiled wearily. "I suspect it is similar in America?"

The image of Brett Cassidy filtered through Bolan's mind.

"You're right there, Commander," he said.

"I think, Agent Cooper, that some rest is advisable. Come, I will show you to a room. You can shower, then sleep. We can talk later over a meal."

The suggestion was the best thing Bolan had heard

for some time. He followed Calberon through the house to a bedroom that had a bathroom attached.

"I will leave you now," Calberon said. "Rest, my friend."

Bolan wandered into the bathroom and turned on the shower. He stood for a long time, letting the water wash over him before he reached for the soap and lathered himself from head to foot. He repeated the procedure a second time before he actually felt clean. His face and body reminded him of the treatment Manolo's men had meted out. He glanced down and saw the darkening, discolored bruising over his ribs and chest, felt the tenderness on his face. There was no feeling sorry for himself as he recalled Maggie Connor's abused body. He had gotten off lightly compared to the journalist.

Out of the shower he toweled himself dry, then returned to the bedroom. He dragged the covers back and fell into bed. Pulling the sheets over him Bolan lay staring at the ceiling, thoughts crowding his mind until exhaustion won out and he fell into a deep sleep.

He woke to brilliant sunlight streaming into the bedroom. Swinging his legs out of bed he padded to the bathroom and took another shower. This time cool water swept away the remaining cobwebs from his mind. Back in the bedroom he saw that someone had laid out clean clothes for him. He dressed, feeling ready to continue his mission. Running his fingers through his damp hair he wandered out of the bedroom and found the living area.

Calberon was there. He turned at Bolan's approach, smiling when he saw the clean clothing.

"I took the liberty of disposing of your other clothes."

Bolan nodded. "Thanks for the new outfit. I guess I must have crashed."

"You slept the day and night through," Calberon said. He showed Bolan to the table. "And woke just in time for breakfast."

"Coffee smells good."

Calberon nodded. "Colombian coffee. And here are scrambled eggs. Scallions and tomato. *Calentado*. That is beans and rice. Please sit down, Agent Cooper."

"Call me Matt."

"José, then, please."

Calberon smiled. As Bolan took a seat at the table he glanced around. They were alone.

"The others are out on assignment," Calberon explained as he filled a cup with rich, dark coffee for Bolan. "It gives us time to talk."

"Do you feel safe here?" Bolan asked.

Calberon raised his hands in acknowledgment of the question.

"I am aware of our vulnerability. It is why we change our location frequently. We have only been here a week and may move on again."

"Must make it hard on your men."

Calberon shrugged. "There is no other choice for us. As long as we pursue Manolo and his kind we are in danger. Manolo alone would wipe us out if he could. The man has no pity. If you have dealt with him you will understand this."

"I understand," Bolan said. "Manolo uses death and the threat of death to get what he wants. It's how he stays on top."

"We work on the same principle. I have told my men

it is how they must deal with the traffickers. There must be no quarter. They have to face the same treatment they give out to others. There is no communication with them. No compromise." The Colombian stared across the table at Bolan. "All the time I tell myself I am doing the right thing."

"Time comes when direct action is the only option. You fight these people on their own terms, or they'll walk right over you and keep going."

"Put aside the law and revert to the ways of the jungle? The survival of right against wrong?"

"Close enough."

Calberon broke off some bread and handed it to Bolan. They concentrated on the food for a while before Calberon spoke again.

"So, Matt Cooper, what can I do to help you?"

"Do you have any intel on Manolo and his contacts? Anyone I might be able to identify? Maybe some you haven't put names to?"

"I will show you what we have."

Calberon produced a file. He laid it on the table and spread out a number of photographic images. Bolan scanned them. He identified Santiago, pointing him out to Calberon.

"You can scratch him from your list. He's dead," the Executioner said.

"Santiago? Manolo's chief enforcer?"

"Not anymore. Santiago was responsible for a triple murder in Miami. He also ran the interrogation that killed Maggie Connor and worked on me, too."

"Good riddance." Calberon tapped another picture. "This one we do not know."

"Cuban government minister. Santos Perez. Knowing who he is doesn't explain his connection to Manolo. Do you know anything about Major Kirby? An American military man?"

"Kirby? No."

"The weapons I destroyed at Manolo's warehouse included a package of U.S. military weapons and uniforms. Just the kind of deal Kirby would be able to put together. Photographic evidence collected by Maggie Connor shows Kirby in the company of Manolo and others."

"American weapons. A Cuban minister? What else do you have to tell me, Agent Cooper?"

"Nothing that makes any sense right now, but I'm still working on it."

"I suspect you need to return to your country to advance your investigation?"

"Yeah. I need to talk with my people and keep things moving. If Manolo and his group are setting something up, time may be running out."

RAUL MANOLO MADE HIMSELF clear to his people.

"Time is something we don't have. This American has evaded us, vanished. One of our teams has been taken down. We do not have fucking time for this shit."

"Maybe he is getting help," Cabrerro suggested. "He is only one man."

"Have you forgotten what he did to Santiago and the others? The warehouse?" Manolo continued his pacing. "I know now where I went wrong. When he first showed up in Miami I should have had him killed. That was my first mistake. I underestimated him. Now I am paying for that mistake. Send out the instruction to all our people. This man, Cooper, is to be killed on sight. No hesitation. I want that bastard dead."

"Our flight will be ready in a half hour."

Manolo nodded. "Deal with this American, Cabrerro. I have to concentrate on the meeting." He jabbed a finger at the man. "The next time I speak to you I want to hear that Cooper is dead. Not almost dead. Not close to being dead. Dead, Cabrerro. With the lid nailed down on his coffin. After we get to Grand Cayman I want you to return to Miami. Supervise the security at the offices. I have a feeling Cooper might show up there. If he does we should make sure he is made welcome."

13

Florida

The Executioner was back in Miami.

He was on home turf and dressed for the war that had erupted around him. Clad in blacksuit he crouched in shadow and assessed the target area.

Santana, Inc. was Manolo's Miami base.

The building was modest by Miami standards, but it was still impressive. The ground floor was taken up by Santana Nights, a loud and brash club that catered to the Miami party crowd. Pounding music. Expensive food and drink. And the ever-present lure of drugs in the background.

Manolo owned several similar clubs around town.

Bolan had been in place for a few hours, watching and waiting. He had left his own vehicle parked in a quiet spot a distance away from the building. He slung an Uzi round his neck, checked his Beretta and Desert Eagle, then eased into the night shadows and made his approach.

Raul Manolo was in for a rude surprise.

The basement garage was full of cars belonging to the club crowd. He was able to slip inside and thread his way through the rows of vehicles until he reached the access door that admitted visitors to the upper floors. The door was watched over by a man sitting in a booth fitted with state-of-the-art surveillance equipment. Bolan had been watching the booth for some time. He realized the man was one of the team who had confronted him at Paul Sebring's studio. The guy was sporting a badly bruised face and his left hand was bandaged. His injuries had relegated him to security duty.

Bolan approached the booth from the man's blind side. Pressed against the wall, with the booth door on his right, Bolan eased the Beretta 93-R from the shoulder rig, the pistol set for single shot. He took a final look around the garage area, seeing no movement. Leaning forward Bolan gripped the booth door and pushed. It slid open, moving on smooth runners. He followed its progress and the moment it was wide enough to admit him he slid into the booth, the muzzle of the Beretta tracking ahead. He pressed it against the back of the man's skull.

"What the fuck...?"

"Don't talk. I need to get upstairs. You are going to help me. Don't turn around. Make it easy for yourself," Bolan said.

"I let you get inside, Mr. Manolo will cut me into little pieces. You think I'm fucking *loco?* Who the hell are you?"

"You forgot me already? I'm hurt. Last time we met you fell for me in a big way."

Bolan heard the guy exhale as he realized who he was.

"*Cooper?* Manolo has posted you for execution. You are a dead man walking."

"I've got nothing to lose, then. Remember that, pal, because it makes me dangerous to be around."

"Listen to me, *hombre*, if Manolo gets his hands on you…"

"You forgot he already had me and I got away. Took down Santiago and his crew. Manolo is on *my* list now."

As he spoke Bolan's left hand was frisking the man's body. He found a 9 mm Glock in a holster on his belt. Bolan took the pistol and tucked it under his own belt.

The guard ignored the gun pressed against his skull and swiveled his seat around to face Bolan. Up close the injured side of his face was a mess of bruised and scraped flesh. The man stared at Bolan, seeing the still-present marks on the big American's own face.

"Hey, Santiago must have danced on your face, *hombre*."

"Where he went he isn't going to be dancing anymore." Bolan pressed the Beretta's muzzle directly between the man's wide-open eyes. "What do they call you?"

"Tomás. Why?"

"I like to have a name for anyone I kill. Makes it a little more personal. Where's Manolo?"

Tomás shook his head.

"He's not here."

Bolan considered his next move. His gaze passed across the control desk, noting the row of monitors that showed the empty offices on the upper floors. There was also a second bank monitoring the inside of the club, minus the sound.

"Is there access from the club into here?" Bolan asked.

"No. The customers have to leave by the street exit and walk into the garage to get their vehicles."

"How about the office staff?"

"A street entrance alongside the club."

"But that's locked at night?"

"Yeah."

"Security staff inside?"

Tomás hesitated. He gasped when Bolan rapped him alongside the head with the Beretta.

"No games, Tomás. Don't mess with me. I've got a big score to settle with the Manolo organization and right now you're nominated as their representative. Got it?"

Tomás nodded. "Four-man team downstairs in the lobby."

"Uniformed security or Manolo's hired guns?"

"Manolo only trusts his own people."

Bolan filed that away. If his probe went belly-up he was going to be facing Manolo's paid hard men, not ex-cops boosting their pensions.

"Do they stay downstairs? Or make regular sweeps?"

"They check the floors every hour. Cabrerro calls in and lets me know to shut off the alarms. When the patrol is done he calls for me to switch on again."

"When is the next patrol due?"

"Anytime now."

"Okay, Tomás, this is how we do it. When Cabrerro calls, you do as he asks. Patrol over, you acknowledge. But you leave the alarms *off*. Still with me?"

Tomás understood, but Bolan could sense that the man was working away inside his head for some way to outfox his captor.

"No tricks, Tomás. I even smell a trick, the first bullet is for you. That's a promise, and believe me I never go back on a promise."

The telephone buzzed and Tomás reached for it. Bolan laid the Beretta's barrel across the top of his hand.

"I understand Spanish," he said.

Tomás picked up, listened, then answered. He put down the phone, glancing at Bolan. "It's time."

"Do it."

Tomás worked the keys that deactivated the building alarms. Lights flashed on his control panel.

"How long does the check take?"

"Twenty minutes, maybe a half hour."

Bolan nodded. He settled with his back to the booth wall where he could watch Tomás and keep his eyes on the monitor screens.

"Tomás, this could turn out to be the longest thirty minutes of your life."

When the phone rang again Tomás jerked out of his sullen stupor. He reached to pick up the receiver. Bolan heard him acknowledge the instruction that the roving security check had been completed. He put the phone down, turning to stare at Bolan.

"Tell me about the garage. Can you shut it off from the outside?" the Executioner asked.

"Yes. Metal grilles come down to seal the entrance and exit."

"Do it. *Now*."

Tomás turned back to the desk and pressed a couple of buttons. Bolan saw the grilles slide into place.

"The security cameras. Do they record what they see?"

"They record digitally."

"And are there monitor screens in Cabrerro's office like yours?"

"Yes. They get a feed from here."

"I want you to key in the hour previous to the last patrol and play it back."

Tomás frowned. "I don't understand."

"For the next hour, Cabrerro will be watching screens showing a playback, not us in the offices. I think you understand, Tomás. Just do it."

Tomás bent over the keyboard, tapping in the instructions that called up the previous hour's recording. Bolan's ever-present Beretta reminded him he was being closely observed.

"It is ready. I just need to give it the go-ahead."

"Do it," Bolan said, watching the row of monitors. When Tomás keyed the final instruction he noticed a momentary flicker in the images.

"They won't see us now," Tomás said.

"Unlock that access door, Tomás, and then let's move." The Executioner prodded his captive with the Beretta. *"Go."*

14

The elevator took them directly to the suite of offices. As the doors slid open, Bolan, the Beretta in his fist, checked out the wide reception area. He saw chairs for waiting visitors, a curving wood-and-glass reception desk. Lush plants in clay pots dotted the floor. Discreet lighting illuminated the area. He pushed Tomás out of the car.

On the trip up Bolan had pulled plastic restraints from one of his blacksuit pockets and secured his captive's hands behind his back. Tomás had started complaining but one look at the American's grim face advised him to stay silent. Now he moved to the center of the reception area, sensing Bolan close behind, and waited for the man's next order.

"Manolo's office. Let's go."

Tomás led the way. As he approached and passed one of the wall-mounted cameras Tomás glanced up at the lens, wondering if Cabrerro had seen the alert icon yet. The move did not go unnoticed and the Executioner heightened his awareness. He knew he was working on borrowed time.

"Here," Tomás said, standing at a set of glass doors that opened into a spacious office suite that was mostly empty.

Bolan's attention was drawn to the top-grade computer setup on one side of the large, solid teak desk standing near the panoramic window. He guided Tomás to the center of the office and made him lie facedown, away from the desk.

"The first time you move *will* be your last," he advised the man.

Bolan sat behind the desk, his Beretta placed close at hand. He hit the power button to start the computer and switched on the monitor. Then he called Aaron Kurtzman on a secured line. He explained where he was and asked if there was anything they could do to retrieve information from the computer.

The answer came after a couple of minutes. "Key in this string and hit Enter," Kurtzman said.

Bolan followed the instructions and saw on-screen activity as Kurtzman's worm started to infest Manolo's system. The download bar appeared and he saw the block start to fill the horizontal strip. It was slow at first but as the infiltration program increased its hold the download began to speed up.

The screen went blank, then threw up a message informing Bolan the task was done. "Thanks, Bear, I'll be in touch," he said and disconnected the call.

He switched the computer's power off and started to go through the desk, yanking open drawers and tipping the contents across the surface. He got a surprise when he emptied one drawer. As the contents slid into view he recognized a couple of items. He found the wallet he'd been carrying when Manolo's team had taken him down at the motel. His Justice Department badge holder was there, too. Bolan scooped them up and secured them in one of his blacksuit pockets.

The desk yielded little else and Bolan was about to

move on when a folded sheet of newsprint caught his eye. He unfolded the single page from a Miami publication. The date showed it to be a couple of months old. Bolan read the headline: Senator Ryland to Push Ahead with Cuba Initiative.

His ears picked up a familiar sound. It came from beyond the office.

The hiss of an elevator door opening.

Bolan folded the paper in his hands and pocketed it. He snatched the Beretta and slid it back in the shoulder rig. He grasped the Uzi, snapping back the bolt, and as he looked up he saw armed figures fanning out and moving in his direction. There were four of them, carrying submachine guns, with every intention of using them.

Tomás shouted to alert his colleagues to Bolan's presence. A shouted response was followed by a hasty burst of automatic fire that shattered one panel of the glass-fronted office wall. A hail of broken fragments showered the room, raining down on the squirming figure on the floor.

Bolan dropped behind the expansive desk, putting his shoulder to the thick teak and heaving upward. He concentrated his energy into raising it, feeling the weight dig into his flesh. A second burst of gunfire added to his effort. The desk tilted until gravity took over and the desk fell on its side, scattering everything on its surface to the floor. The computer landed hard enough to shatter the monitor. As Bolan sucked in air he heard slugs hammering into the desktop. None came through, allowing him a brief space of time to prepare himself for what was to come. A quick scan of the office behind him and to the sides only confirmed there was no way out.

The only exit was the way he had come in.

More bullets hit the desk, others the floor on either side. The Executioner was being penned in. It was hard fire to keep him undercover while the enemy advanced. It wasn't the first time he'd been in such a situation. Having his back to the wall meant there was only one way to go.

And in doing it he took the battle to the enemy.

The firing ceased for a moment. Bolan picked up movement, the tread of feet on shattered glass. He moved to one side of the upturned desk, leaned around with the Uzi tracking ahead, and spotted the crouching dark figure of an armed man in the act of signaling to someone across from him. Bolan leaned his weight against the desk to steady himself as he swung the Uzi up, triggering a hard burst into the first man. The 9 mm volley hit him in the upper chest, the impact toppling the crouching man on his back. He lay screaming, his feet drumming the carpeted floor as his life ran out.

Bolan heard a muffled curse. The second man was losing control at the sight of his bloodied partner. There was a rush of sound as he pounded across the office floor, firing indiscriminately at the desk shielding Bolan. The slugs thudded into the hard teak with little effect, but gave Bolan an indication where the guy was coming from. He twisted his upper body around and angled the Uzi vertically. He saw the muzzle of the man's weapon an instant before the reckless owner leaned over the edge, his weapon searching for a target. Bolan triggered the Uzi, the harsh rattle of the weapon drowning the guy's startled yell as 9 mm bullets ripped into his throat and shredded his jaw and lower face. His scream of alarm turned to silence as he crashed to the floor on his back.

Bolan rolled to his feet, hot brass casings from the Uzi scattering off his body.

Two down, two to go.

Unless, as well as being a liar, Tomás couldn't count and there were more than four hard men on patrol.

Bolan peered around the edge of the desk. Just beyond the first downed shooter he saw Tomás struggling to climb to his feet. Moving in toward him was another armed man. Tomás started to yell at the guy as he pushed to his knees, his words coming out in an unintelligible torrent.

The man threw an angry glance at Tomás.

Bolan got to his feet, swinging the Uzi, stroking back the trigger and stitching the gunman with a pounding burst of 9 mm slugs. The man gasped from the impact, slumping to his knees. He struggled to raise his own weapon. The Uzi's second burst centered over his heart and put him down on the carpeted floor.

Moving out from behind the desk Bolan ran forward, positioning himself behind the jutting pillar at the edge of the office entrance. He heard the sound of an automatic pistol, felt the vibration as the heavy caliber slug slammed into the pillar, spitting plaster fragments. The shot had come from across the reception area. Bolan spied a soft gleam of light shining on a brass casing on the carpet at the far end of the reception desk.

Target spotted.

Bolan ejected his magazine and snapped in a fresh one, cocking the Uzi.

He picked up movement close by.

Tomás.

The man was on his feet, anger twisting his dark

features as he took a lunging run at the Executioner, shouting more warnings to the remaining guard. He used his left shoulder to batter Bolan as he closed the gap.

From the corner of his eye Bolan spotted the guard rising from cover, his big pistol starting to level.

"Come on, Cabrerro, shoot the fuck," Tomás shouted.

Cabrerro triggered a shot that seared a burning line across Bolan's right cheek.

Bolan returned fire, his 9 mm volley scoring the top of the reception desk, causing Cabrerro to jerk back.

Still yelling Tomás lunged at Bolan again. The Executioner turned and slammed the solid weight of the Uzi into the man's face. The blow landed hard and Tomás crashed to the floor. He made another attempt to grab at Bolan as he moved past. Bolan slammed the heel of his boot into Tomás's throat.

Bolan let momentum carry him forward, executing a drop roll that took him across the carpeted floor. He heard the boom of Cabrerro's handgun, the big slug passing over him at waist height. He straightened his body, jerking the Uzi front and center, triggering the weapon. He held the Uzi steady, the muzzle angled up at the bulk of Cabrerro's body, catching him hip first, then arcing the weapon to lay the rest of the long burst into the man's soft torso. Cabrerro stumbled back against the desk, clawing at the shiny surface as he tried to stay upright. The damage from Bolan's hot fire was too severe and he slumped, spilling to his knees and flopping in a bloody mess at the base of the reception desk. His forgotten pistol slipped from his hand, thudding to the floor.

Bolan climbed to his feet, body aching from his desperate actions. The sting of the bullet burn across his cheek reminded him he was still alive. Behind him he heard a soft, continuous moaning. Bolan glanced to where Tomás sprawled motionless. Blood had poured from his battered face, pooling in a thick spread beneath his head. The Executioner turned away, crossing the reception area. He stood over Cabrerro. The man raised his head slowly, his eyes still angry as he stared up at the black-clad figure towering over him.

"Manolo will gut you like a fish on a slab," the Colombian said, forcing the words between his bloody lips.

"I'm getting tired of being told what your boss is going to do," Bolan said. "Take a look around, Cabrerro. He hasn't done too well up to now. Maybe it's because I'm not defenseless like Maggie Connor. And I'm not finished yet. If you live long enough, tell him I'm still coming for him and *Paso Trasero* isn't going to happen."

15

Cayman Islands

The news reached Raul Manolo in the early hours. He had been in bed for just over an hour when Costa came to his room and told him what had happened in Miami.

"How many dead?"

"Cabrerro and his team."

"Cabrerro?"

"Cabrerro. And Tomás."

Manolo took a deep breath.

"Later I have the meeting with the others. I need to focus on that. Costa, I want you to arrange something for me. Contact Victor Capstone. Offer him a contract on Cooper. I want that man dead. Goddamn it, I want his fucking head delivered in a basket. Do it. Make Capstone an offer he will find impossible to refuse."

WHEN LUIS COSTA BOARDED the two-hundred-foot motor cruiser *La Perla* he was ready to relax. Over the past day he had flown to Miami, had his meet with Victor Capstone, then flown back to Grand Cayman. He had been picked up at the airport and driven to the marina where a sleek launch had ferried him out to Manolo's boat, anchored offshore. As he stepped onto the immaculate deck one of the armed security crew came out to meet him.

"He wants to see you now," the guy said, shrugging his broad shoulders in sympathy.

Costa followed the guard to the stateroom on the middle deck. Stepping inside he saw Manolo sitting on a tall stool at the curving teak-and-chrome wet bar, a tall glass in one big hand. Manolo looked cool and at ease in white slacks and a blue shirt. He filled a second glass and held it out as Costa approached.

"Luis, you look like crap on legs."

Costa took the glass, raising it in a salute. "Thank you, *Jefe,* that is just what I need after today."

"How did it go?"

"Everything is set. Capstone is onboard."

Costa took a long swallow from the glass, letting the cool liquor wet his dry throat.

"I knew I was right sending you to deal with him. Make sure he gets more than just standard expenses. He's the best in the business." Manolo raised his glass. "To Cooper. May he rot in hell."

They emptied their glasses. Costa refused a second.

"You sure?" Manolo asked. "Go and take it easy. Just be on time for dinner tonight."

"How is it going?" Costa asked.

"We are about to make the final arrangements for a greeting Senator Ryland would surely appreciate if he was still alive after the event."

"Have you heard from Kirby yet?"

"A little while ago. The replacement weapons have been organized. Shipment arrives late tomorrow."

"Good."

Manolo slapped him on the back. "Go and rest up. Do not forget dinner. Eight sharp."

Manolo returned to the main salon where his guests were assembled. They had been there for the past few hours, discussing the operation and going over details.

With the arrival of Costa, Manolo had called a brief adjournment, arranging for fresh coffee and anything else the gathering might want. The members of the consortium had to be prepared to disrupt the planned meeting between Senator Paul Ryland and representatives of the Cuban government.

As he entered the controlled temperature of the glass-walled salon Manolo saw white-coated waiters laying out the fine buffet. He waited until they had withdrawn before he spoke.

"You will be pleased to know that the Cooper problem has been contracted out to someone who used to be a shooter for the SAS. It will allow us to concentrate on the business at hand."

Manolo waved a hand in the direction of the food. "Please relax and help yourselves. The man I've hired is the best there is."

He headed toward the food. Chico Delgado joined him, filling a plate.

"Hey, this is good, Raul. I might have to poach your chef."

Manolo glanced at him. "Chico, I still have the SAS man's number."

There was a slight smile on his lips. Delgado grinned weakly. He hadn't failed to notice the smile did not lessen the cold expression in Manolo's eyes. He held up his hands in mock surrender.

"Only joking," he said.

"Me, too," Manolo replied and walked away to take his seat at the conference table.

Delgado felt the faint chill the man left behind. He frowned a little, shook off the feeling and returned to his own seat.

When everyone had satisfied their appetites they settled down with coffee. Cigars were passed around.

"Are we all familiar with the timetable?" Manolo asked. The nods of affirmation pleased him. "Good. Our teams will be in place by midday of the meeting. If there are any last-minute changes, Cassidy, will your man be able to inform us in time?"

"No problem." Cassidy smiled. "He does exactly what I tell him."

"Let's hope it remains so," Santos Perez said.

Brett Cassidy was not impressed with the man. The Cuban government minister had a slightly superior attitude that left a barrier between him and those he considered beneath him. Perez pointedly chose to ignore the fact that he was as corrupt as anyone he maligned. He had made a fortune out of his dirty dealings, including drug trafficking via Manolo, and was still raking in money and favors from his other operations.

If the proposed meeting between Senator Ryland and the Cuban delegates had a fruitful outcome, and a degree of cooperation and increased trading took place, much of the need for backdoor dealing would evaporate. Perez would lose some of his negotiating power and along with it his illicit income. The man, a politician through and through, made a lot of noise on the subject of his loyalty to the Marxist line. He claimed to stand with the rank and file, always there to fly the flag, but behind the dogma he was only interested in his own profits.

"I said he was okay, Perez. That means he is. Make sure your end of the deal holds up and leave me to handle mine," Cassidy said.

Perez glared at the American, his feelings almost getting the better of him. He kept his temper, turning aside and concentrating on preparing and lighting the fine cigar Manolo had offered him. When this was all over and things were as they should be, perhaps he might have time arrange for something to happen to Cassidy. The man, like many Americans, had a bad attitude. His arrogance, and his self-assured stance when he spoke to Perez, made the Cuban seethe inside. The way he called him *Perez*, disregarding the ministerial title, was Cassidy's way of ignoring rank and ascendance. But his day would come, and on that day Cassidy would learn the hardest lesson of all and pay with his life.

"Friends," Manolo said, smiling, "let's put our efforts into making sure this operation works for everyone. We will all gain from its success. Each of us, for different reasons, wants *Paso Tresero* to succeed. Right now it is all that really matters. Nothing else must get in the way."

AFTER THE MEETING Manolo took Cassidy aside.

"I want you back in Miami. There is something I need you to do. Now that Kirby has delivered I feel his involvement can be terminated."

Cassidy nodded. "Understood. One less wild card to worry about. And I can check on our FBI buddy. Keep him on his toes."

"I'll leave the details about Kirby to you. Just make sure that any solution you come up with involves closing his mouth permanently."

16

Florida

"I poked around in Manolo's accounts after we downloaded from his computer. That guy has some system there. Everything is linked back to the main bank in the Caymans. Even his Swiss accounts. And somebody has been playing very cleverly. Switching payments, running dummy accounts, creating nonexistent business fronts. Do you have any idea the sort of money we're talking here? This guy is loaded," Aaron Kurtzman said.

"That's why they run their operations the way they do. Money is no object. Let's them buy whatever, or whoever, they want," the Executioner replied.

"Yeah? Well, one of them isn't as sharp as he should have been. I picked up regular payments to what turned out to be a cover account drawn on a bank in London. Over time that account had built up nicely. When I got into the system it appears someone had been making transfers to a bank in Virginia. A few thousand here and there. Not the big amounts you would expect from someone associated with Manolo. So I accessed the account details for the Virginia end and got a name. Ran it and guess what? Came up with a real, live FBI agent. Name of Trilling. Vincent Trilling. He works out of the Miami field office."

"Raul Manolo and an FBI agent. And we've got Brett Cassidy in the frame, as well."

"Some mix, Striker. How are you going to play this?"

"See if I can get to Trilling. How good are you at hacking into his account and emptying it? Moving the money so he can't get hold of it?"

"Shouldn't be a problem. Give me a little bit of time."

Kurtzman called back in just under two hours. Considering what he had set out to achieve that was impressive as far as Bolan was concerned. The call confirmed that Vincent Trilling's bank accounts had been accessed and his assets stripped and placed in hidden and protected accounts known only to Kurtzman.

"When Trilling finds out, he is going to be one unhappy FBI bunny," Kurtzman said. "Even more when he contacts his banks and they tell him they have no idea what happened or where his money has gone."

TRILLING WAS OFF DUTY, at his Miami apartment, when his cell phone began to ring.

"Vince Trilling. Who's this?"

"Check your bank accounts, Agent Trilling. I'll wait." The male voice was calm, commanding.

"What the hell...?"

"You're wasting time, Trilling," the caller interrupted. "Check your accounts. The one on the mainland and the Cayman Islands account."

Trilling felt weak. He put down the cell and went to his computer. He entered the code for the Cayman Islands account he thought no one knew existed. When it came on-screen he ran down the column until he was presented with the current balance.

Every dollar he had in the account was gone. He rechecked. The entire amount had been withdrawn, leaving him with nothing. Trilling sat staring at the screen, the feeling of despair in his stomach beginning to grow. Hastily he logged out and went into his mainland account. It was the same. The money was gone. He had been cleaned out.

Trilling snatched up his phone, sweat already forming on his face.

"What the fuck is going on?"

"I know where the money came from."

The caller disconnected.

Trilling was not sure how much time went by. He sat with the phone in his hand, his gaze centered on the screen of his laptop.

His money was all gone.

Trilling didn't know what else to do so he made a call himself. It was the second time he had called the special number that day. The first time had been to pass along information that was vital to his employer. Now he was calling with something vital to his future.

Raul Manolo listened with mounting irritation. He concealed his feelings from the caller. When Trilling had finished he asked a simple question.

"Did you say anything about our deal?"

"No. Why would I do that, Mr. Manolo? I respect your privacy. I'm just concerned the FBI might have a hand in this. Maybe they found out what I've been doing. Mr. Manolo—Raul—I need your help. I think you…owe me."

"Vincent, don't worry. Calm down. I'll deal with this. Do something for me. Stay in your apartment until I get back to you. I'll make the arrangements the minute

I put the phone down. Like you say, Vincent, this could affect us both. So things need to be done quickly. I'll call you right back."

Manolo made another phone call.

"Eduardo, take three men with you. Pick up Vincent Trilling at his apartment. Do it quietly until you have him in your vehicle. Subdue him and drive out to the Everglades. You know where to take him. Make that FBI bastard realize he has outlived his usefulness, then leave him for the alligators." Manolo recalled what Trilling had said. "He thinks the FBI may be on to him. I don't want him spilling his guts to the Feds. That little shit had the nerve to tell me I *owe* him."

Eduardo nodded. "He won't bother you again, *Jefe*."

Manolo had one more call to make before he'd feel satisfied.

"Cassidy, it seems our friend Trilling has been compromised. He's already given me the information we need but since then it appears his involvement may have been picked up by the authorities. I have dispatched a team to deal with him."

"I'm on my way to handle Kirby. Let me know if I can help later."

"I'm sure this can be resolved easily," Manolo said. "You concentrate on our military man. Retire him quickly."

THE EXECUTIONER PICKED UP the call from Stony Man Farm. He listened to the information from Kurtzman. In simple terms, they had been monitoring Vincent Trilling's cell phone. Precisely, his call to Manolo.

"Moving his money has made the guy jumpy. Telling

Manolo has just put him on the at-risk list," Bolan said. "Trilling has just become a disposable item. He knows too much. Manolo isn't going to want him able to talk to save his own skin."

"You about to make a house call?" Kurtzman asked.

"I'd better before Manolo makes one of his own."

BOLAN HIT THE STREET where Trilling had his apartment and saw four men escorting the man out of the building and into a silver SUV. The first impression was that Trilling was going with them voluntarily. Gut instinct warned Bolan it wasn't the case.

Trilling climbed into the backseat with two of the men. The vehicle pulled away from the building and merged with the traffic. Bolan followed, a couple of cars behind. His mind worked on a number of possible scenarios, none of them affording him much comfort. Problem one was his inability to help Trilling while they were on the busy street. All he could do for the moment was stay on the SUV's tail, waiting for opportunity to present itself.

The driver knew Miami well. He drove at a steady pace, west through the city, until the urban sprawl dropped behind them and they started picking up signs for the highway.

That would take them away from the city, in the direction of the Everglades.

Busy traffic on the westbound highway allowed Bolan to trail the SUV. He maintained his distance, never once losing sight of the silver vehicle. When it finally took an off-ramp, Bolan allowed his own speed to drop, ignoring the impatient blaring of horns. He eased into the exit lane and merged with the ramp, following its curve to the adjoining road. He was able to see the SUV already speeding along the black ribbon a distance ahead. He dropped into position well behind.

After a few miles Bolan saw they were well into the wetlands, with the watery Everglades stretching away on either side of the road. There were wide spreads of thick saw grass and reeds, and stands of cyprus trees, the trunks covered in Spanish moss. It was home to abundant wildlife—the predatory alligator, soft-moving cottonmouth snakes.

Today another predator had invaded the silent wilderness.

Vincent Trilling was the human prey.

The Executioner knew Manolo's victim would be taken to an isolated spot, killed and dumped in the water for the ever-present alligators. It was a workable, but grisly, method of problem solving.

Up ahead the vehicle's windows caught light as it made a sudden left turn off the road. Bolan hit the gas pedal, closing the distance to the spot where he had seen the SUV disappear. He might still have missed the turn if he hadn't spotted the thin mist of dust in the motionless air and noted the crushed grass. Checking the area he saw the break in the tall plants that marked the entrance to a side trail.

Bolan kept his speed to a crawl, aware he was placing himself in a vulnerable position. Despite his caution he kept going. Somewhere ahead Trilling was being led closer to his death. If Bolan failed to reach him he would lose any information the FBI man might have.

He saw the trail curving in toward the water. His

senses told him Manolo's men would be reaching their chosen place soon. He decided it was time he exited his vehicle and moved in on foot. He braked the SUV. Bolan slipped off his jacket. He carried the Beretta 93-R in its shoulder rig. He grabbed a lightweight combat harness, pouches holding additional magazines for the Beretta and magazines for the Uzi. The Executioner opened his door and stepped out, moving off along the trail.

He picked up voices only minutes later, off to his left, where the grass grew taller than his head. Bolan saw the tracks where Manolo's men had swerved away from the trail. Now the voices were louder. He heard laughter, too. And the sound of blows. Someone grunting in pain.

Bolan set the Uzi, easing through the thick grasses, working his way to the tight grouping of trees that shielded his approach. He got close enough and was able to see Manolo's four heavies surrounding Vincent Trilling. The FBI agent's hands were bound in front of him. One of the men was holding up a knife and waving it in Trilling's bloody face.

The Executioner stormed out of the trees full tilt, his weapon up and firing, sending streams of 9 mm slugs into the bodies of the snatch team. The knife holder went down first and Bolan was left with three to take out.

The Uzi was crackling in a steady burst that hit the trio, even as they went for their holstered weapons. Bolan was in no mood for compromise. His initial scan of the scene had shown him the pitiful condition of the man the Manolo crew had snatched. Trilling, barely able to stand on his own feet, his front streaked with blood, had offered no resistance when the man had threatened him with a knife. It was as if everything had been knocked out of him as he stared with dulled eyes at his captors.

The 9 mm slugs punctured flesh and shattered bone, knocking the targets back, stunned expressions on their faces as they absorbed the heavy fire from the Uzi. They had not been expecting any kind of challenge. This was *their* deal. They worked for Raul Manolo, and Manolo went unchallenged.

With the Executioner in the equation, things had changed. Now Manolo was facing aggression. His men and his property were under threat.

Bolan's way was in direct opposition to Manolo's plan. There was an obstinate determination in his refusal to bow down to Manolo and his people.

As the last man standing stumbled in response to the power of the Uzi, Bolan eased off the trigger. He dropped the spent magazine and replaced it with a full one. He never once took his eyes off the downed crew, his attention fully absorbed until he assured himself they posed no further threat.

Only then did he turn to Vincent Trilling.

The rogue FBI man was still on his feet, looking around with a blend of fear and total surprise etched across his bruised and bloody face. He stared, taking in the bodies sprawled on the ground. He was looking at the end results of violence and sudden death. Bolan could see it had been a shock to Trilling's system. This was all new to the man. He most likely had never seen death this close up. Bolan hoped the shock would make Trilling start talking. He had saved the man's life—he owed him little else.

Trilling was a betrayer of his FBI legacy. The story

was far from new. Trilling had sold out for money. One of the oldest excuses for turning against everything he had sworn to uphold.

In his FBI work Trilling must have investigated crimes of a similar nature. So he knew the risks, understood the odds against succeeding. Yet like so many before him he had decided he would be the exception. The one who could get away with the crime. Bolan might have understood if Trilling had been a civilian. But as a professional law officer he had made his decision, let down his colleagues and proved his utter lack of credibility. He was about to find he had a lot to answer for.

The FBI wanted him.

And so did Manolo's hit squads.

Mack Bolan would risk his life to keep the man alive by putting his own life on the line. But he wanted some answers.

Trilling sensed a change in Bolan's stance as the big man moved toward him. His bound hands rose in a half-hearted defensive action as Bolan closed in. He might as well have been attempting to stop a battle tank, his reaction ignored as the man in black reached out a large hand and bunched the front of Trilling's bloody shirt. Bolan pulled Trilling toward him, then slammed him back against the SUV hard enough to hurt. Trilling wrapped his hands around Bolan's wrist, trying to loosen his grip. Bolan shook the FBI man as if he was a rag doll. Then he pressed his Beretta against Trilling's cheek, drawing a shocked gasp from the man.

"One chance, Trilling. I'm going to ask a question and if you lie I'll finish what Manolo's crew started. I can walk away from this and no one will know I've been here.

Don't insult me by trying to smart talk your way out. You have two options. Being dead or going to prison. Personally I don't give a damn which one you choose."

Trilling's panic showed. He knew his dream of a wealthy retirement had slipped away. Bolan had read the man right. Vincent Trilling was too much of a coward to choose a quick death.

"What the hell do you want?" he asked slowly, every word hurting as he delivered it from his battered mouth.

"I want to know what Back Step is. Just what Manolo and his friends are planning and when it's going down. Make the right choice, Trilling, because the clock is ticking."

"Then get me to a hospital first. Please. They kicked me bad when I was down. Feels like they broke something inside. Jesus, it hurts. Get me a hospital and protection. Then I'll tell you everything."

17

Florida

Victor Capstone had already checked out possible kill zones. Aware that his target was operating within Manolo's territory enabled him to search within a defined area. He'd been notified that Cooper was hitting Manolo's Miami base. He concentrated his search for Cooper's presence, accepting that the man was no amateur himself. Cooper had the ability to move quickly, infiltrate security and take down his targets with a thoroughness Capstone admired.

And Cooper was taking no prisoners. First the warehouse in Valledupar, then the office setup in Miami. Cooper was waging a war of attrition against his adversary, wearing them down by striking indiscriminately, moving on, then hitting again while the enemy was still reeling. Capstone knew that having his power base reduced little by little had an unsettling effect on Manolo. It revealed that, despite his power, his influence and his overwhelming feeling of being in control, the kingpin would begin to lose some of his status. Feeling unsettled could lead to mistakes being made.

Where would Cooper strike next?

Capstone scanned the list of likely places, working

a process of elimination. Certain locations were too small, unimportant, so Cooper was less likely to be concerned with those. He crossed them off the list.

His phone rang. It was Luis Costa.

"I am in-flight. I will be in Miami in an hour. We need to meet. Same location as last time."

"Fine. You must be collecting some serious frequent flyer miles."

Capstone ended the call. He leaned back in his seat, gazing out the balcony doors. He sensed another contract showing over the horizon. Logic told him it had to do with Manolo's business, and in that case there would be a link to Cooper. He found himself grinning. Capstone had no problem with that. He glanced at his watch. Plenty of time to go before Costa showed his face. He could shower and change into fresh clothing, take himself down to the bar and have a drink. Why not? It all went on Raul Manolo's tab.

LUIS COSTA FOUND Capstone in a chair facing the entrance to the lobby. Crossing to meet him Costa sat down himself. Capstone raised a finger and ordered drinks when the waiter came over.

"Luis, you look like you need a long vacation."

"Tell me about it. But this is a busy time for us."

"Whatever you lot have going I hope it's worth the effort you're all putting in."

Costa waited until his drink had been delivered. He took a long swallow. "You do not know half," he said.

"Mate, I don't know shit. And it isn't my business. Manolo is a client. I don't pry. Not a wise thing to do in my line of work."

Costa nodded and handed a folder to Capstone. Inside were two printed sheets of data and a couple of photographs.

"His name is Victor Trilling. He's FBI. Local field office. Into intelligence gathering. Until now he's been selling us information," Costa said.

"What changed?"

"Someone got to him. Scared him so much he called Manolo and put pressure on him to help. Manolo decided to help him into the next life. A team grabbed Trilling and drove him out to the Everglades. Apparently they were followed. Our men were wiped out and Trilling was rescued. The bodies of the team were found near where they would have dumped Trilling."

"Nicely explained," Capstone said. "Do we assume the white knight was our old chum Cooper?"

Costa nodded. "Our contact in the police department confirmed that a Lieutenant Gary Loomis took a call from Cooper. It seems Cooper had a witness he needed protecting in the hospital where he was getting treatment. Loomis took a couple of his squad and they're at the hospital now, along with Cooper. We would like it if Trilling didn't survive his visit."

The look on Capstone's face told Costa the man was not happy with the setup.

"Mr. Manolo is aware this is an unusual request. He appreciates you prefer more time to prepare for a job."

"Too bleedin' right, mate. A quick fix like this is risky. No situation recon. I need a shooting point that gives me cover and lets me get clear with time to spare. Going in cold goes against every rule I ever set for myself."

"We understand what we're asking is extreme. But

the situation calls for drastic measures. Mr. Manolo is willing to pay well above your normal fee. I am authorized to offer you…this." Costa slid a folded paper from his pocket and handed it to the British hitman. "If you accept I make a call and the money will be transferred to your account within the next few minutes."

Capstone opened the paper and looked at the amount. He cleared his throat and took a long drink from his glass.

"You're quite certain there aren't too many zeros on that number?" It was the only question he was able to come up with at that moment.

"It's correct," Costa said.

Capstone checked the amount again. If he collected the fee he would be able to retire the very next day. He could buy his own Caribbean island to retire to. He took a moment to consider his options. He would be risking his life, his reputation, and breaking every rule he had ever set for himself.

But the size of the fee was impossible to ignore. Victor Capstone was no coward. He had never walked away from difficult situations in his life. His SAS experience had trained him to control fear and calculate the odds of any given scenario. Preplanning was always advised, but there were times when instant reaction was necessary, and staying put could mean allowing an opportunity to slip away. The SAS had their famous motto: Who Dares Wins. It was imprinted on the subconscious of every man who took on the challenge of the regiment. Capstone still based his actions on that motto. Do nothing, you gained nothing. If he walked away from Manolo's offer, regardless of the risk, he would carry the memory for the rest of his life and call himself every kind of fool for turning it down.

"What the hell," he said softly, then raised his voice. "Go ahead, Luis, make that call."

Costa took out his phone and spoke in rapid Spanish. He listened to a response, nodding once before he shut down the call.

"It is done. If you wish I will wait for you to confirm the transfer to your account."

"I trust you, Luis. Now, I need as much information as you can give me on the hospital. Room and floor number. Any updates." Capstone paused. "You said Miami police are involved. What about the FBI? Isn't it normal for them to deal with one of their own?"

Costa shrugged. "I can only assume Cooper wants Trilling under his control until he can extract information. Once the FBI is called in it would exclude everyone *not* FBI."

"Let your inside man have my cell number. I'll want instant updating if things change," the contract killer said.

"You will have it."

They parted company, Costa leaving the hotel, Capstone returning to his room.

From deep in the walk-in closet he took out a locked case. He placed it on the bed, keyed in the lock combinations and opened it.

He took out his Barrett M-82 rifle. The .50 caliber semiautomatic was Capstone's chosen sniper weapon. It had served him well for many years. Since he had obtained the rifle he had worked on it, improving and honing its performance to suit his own needs. He knew the rifle intimately, knew its capabilities, and trusted it to perform. The .50 caliber cartridges he used were handmade to fine tolerances. He measured out the powder to the last grain, checking and weighing each finished bullet to make sure it met his requirements. If it didn't it was scrapped. He needed bullets that would fly true, staying within trajectory as they rose and fell so that target acquisition was maintained. The proof his efforts were worthwhile showed in a one-hundred percent kill score. By always being prepared, Capstone never missed.

He checked the weapon over. It was coated in a nonreflective matte black finish. He picked up the optic scope and clicked it in place. He secured the scope, walking to the balcony, and leaned against the frame for support. He raised the rifle and looked through the scope. It was set and calibrated. Capstone scanned the bay, bringing into focus a far-distant windsurfer. The surfer's image was magnified to show fine detail. Satisfied, Capstone returned to the bed.

He picked up one of a number of loaded magazines, weighing it in his hand. His usual load was the five-round clip. He had always worked on the premise that if he couldn't hit his target within five shots, then it wouldn't matter. With the possibility of a second target this time—Trilling and maybe even Cooper—he chose a ten-round magazine. Clipped inside the lid of the rifle case was a Glock 20 handgun and three 10 mm, fifteen-round clips. Capstone examined the pistol, working the slide and dry firing a couple of times to make sure there were no problems. He clicked in a magazine, cocked the weapon and returned it to its clip, then replaced the rifle. In the bottom of the case, secured by Velcro straps were a couple of smoke canisters. Another of Capstone's emergency backups. He closed the case, locked it and placed it on the floor beside the bed.

Capstone crossed to the suite's minibar and helped

himself to a soft drink from the cooler. He stayed away from any form of alcohol once he began preparing for a hit. He needed his senses sharp. The criteria for his long-distance shooting required him to be accurate within very fine tolerances and anything liable to blur that accuracy was not allowed. He thought about the drink he'd had in the hotel lobby with Costa. He'd never have consumed it if he'd known the plan was going to change. Again, he felt some concern about deviating in any way from his normal operating procedure.

He sat in a chair and waited for the call from Costa, or one of his people, that would give him his location. Once he had that he would move. Capstone was aware he might be working within a short time span. He understood that, and despite his reluctance to break his self-imposed rules, he only had to remember the prodigious fee Manolo had offered.

"What the hell, Victor, even you can't live forever," he said.

When the cell phone rang, the caller identified himself as Costa's man. He gave Capstone a concise rundown on the detail he had. Capstone absorbed the information and ended the call. He pushed to his feet, slipped on a light jacket and picked up his rifle case. Leaving the hotel suite he made his way to the closest elevator and rode the car to the basement garage. His rental car, a plain, unobtrusive Ford, had been chosen for its anonymity. Capstone placed the case in the trunk, started the motor and drove to the exit. His key card opened the gate. He took the car onto the street, turning east, and followed the traffic flow.

It took twenty minutes to reach the vicinity of the

hospital. Capstone drove until he was on the side of the four-story building where Victor Trilling's room was located. From there he drove on, cutting along a cross street that would take him away from the hospital but allow him to keep the target area in sight. He found what he was looking for within a few minutes. He drove until he located the entrance to the multistory parking garage that would suit his needs. It was a self-service operation so he paused at the barrier and pressed for a ticket. When the barrier rose Capstone drove through and followed the ramps until he finally emerged on the rooftop level. There were only three other vehicles there. He parked in a slot that would allow him to look across the intervening buildings toward the hospital complex. He stepped out of the car and checked out the roof. In the center was a large block structure that enclosed the elevator machinery. It stood around fourteen feet high and the top of the structure, some twenty feet square, bristled with outlet ducts. It was ideal for him to prepare his fire base.

Capstone made his way across to the structure. Around the far side was a metal ladder fixed to the wall. He climbed up, dropped over the raised lip and hauled his rifle case as he worked his way to the side facing his target. A quick check confirmed there were no buildings in the vicinity tall enough to expose him. He opened his case, removed the Glock pistol and laid it close by. Then he took out the Barrett and unfolded the short legs fixed beneath the fore barrel housing. He snapped in a ten-round magazine, made sure the scope was secure, then stretched out in a firing position. He raised the rifle, snugging it to his shoulder, and peered through the scope. Working the focus ring snapped the distant blur of the hospital into sharp relief. He used the telephoto facility to bring the image even closer, counting off the floors and the windows until he fixed on the room where Trilling was being held.

The figures inside the room were clearly visible.

There was a man in the hospital bed, propped up on pillows. Capstone smiled as he recognized Victor Trilling, despite the fact his face was bruised and swollen. Capstone could see his lips moving, slowly, as if speaking was causing him extreme pain.

Standing at the foot of the bed was a second figure. *Cooper.*

A third man leaned against the wall, arms folded, his interest fixed on the conversation between Cooper and Trilling. His open jacket revealed the badge clipped to his belt. From the information Capstone had received, the man would be a Miami-Dade police officer.

Capstone settled into his prone position, body and legs configuring the shooting stance that would offer him the ideal solid base for firing. He worked the cocking mechanism, feeding the first round into the chamber, hands curling around the rifle. He eased the muzzle around until he had Victor Trilling in his sights and adjusted for drift and trajectory, allowing for distance and curvature. Capstone did all this without conscious effort. He was coming into his own now, working the skills he had acquired over the years. He made a fine adjustment to the scope, mentally allowing for the foreshortened image, calculating the differential in his mind.

Victor Trilling's head was in the crosshairs for a brief

moment before Capstone raised the muzzle a degree or two, compensating for the length of the flight.

His finger eased back on the trigger, knowing exactly how much pressure he needed to make a clean shot. His thoughts cleared.

All he saw, all he considered, was his target.

There was nothing else in Capstone's mind as he completed his trigger pull.

18

Trilling, back from treatment, was still groggy from the anesthetic he had been given. He had four badly broken ribs down his right side and two on the left. His left arm had a fracture below the elbow. He'd lost a couple of teeth and his jaw had been pushed out of its socket. He was covered in heavy bruising and his right eye was swollen shut.

Bolan and Loomis had been waiting when Trilling was returned to his room. The MDPD had uniformed officers patrolling the hospital and there were two officers posted outside the FBI agent's room.

While they waited the Executioner had outlined the events that had brought them to the current situation.

"I was wondering what had happened to you," Loomis said, staring at Bolan's unshaven and bruised face. "You sure you should be up and around?"

"Until I figure this out I don't have any alternative."

"Hey, I'll do what I can to help," Loomis said.

"Thanks. Right now we need to keep Trilling under watch. And I need to get him to tell me what the hell is going on."

"How long can we keep his FBI buddies from storming in and snatching him back?"

"Once I have my answers they're welcome to him."

"Cooper, I've got to say this. Word on the street is Manolo has been hit a couple of times. A bunch of his people were taken down. It's the talk of the precinct, too."

Bolan's expression was one of total innocence as he looked across at the cop.

"I heard that, too."

"Son of a bitch," Loomis said, grinning. "Where is the dirtbag right now?"

"That's something I'm hoping Agent Trilling can tell us."

"That's encouraging. You said tell *us*."

"Loomis, I'm not deliberately keeping you in the dark."

"Considering the way you operate it might be the best idea. That way I might keep my job."

Trilling was coming around and the nurses had left the room.

"Payback time, Trilling," the Executioner said. "You got your hospital and your protection."

Trilling stared at him, his expression sullen. He licked at dry, swollen lips.

"What if I change my mind?"

Bolan glanced at Loomis. The Miami cop shrugged.

"Let's go," Loomis said. "My men have better things to do than protect this traitor."

"Just remember one thing," Bolan added. "Raul Manolo is not going to forget about you. You're here because he wanted to kill you. Who you want to take a chance with is up to you. Your choice, Trilling."

Trilling grimaced. There was no easy option, but he wanted to stay alive.

"If I talk to you I'm headed for jail time."

"Alive you can try for a deal," Bolan said.

Trilling thought about that. Struggling against pain he looked at the big man standing beside his bed. Cooper had followed his end of the bargain. He'd hauled Trilling out of the Everglades to his car and brought him to this hospital. He'd even arranged for the police to stand watch over him. He could imagine what they thought about him. An FBI agent turned dirty. Selling information to Raul Manolo.

"Manolo wanted verification on the date for the meeting between Senator Ryland and a delegation from the Cuban government."

"The peace accord?" Loomis asked.

"Certain parties in Cuba don't want any easing of the tension between Cuba and the U.S. Make trade legal they'll lose millions in black-market dealing. It would spoil what they've built up over the years. Members of the administration are filling their bank accounts because of the sanctions. They want to hang on to their power, not weaken it. Same goes for the military."

Trilling paused. "They have interest from the U.S., as well. There are people here who want Cuba to stay isolated. They have too much to lose if we go soft on the Cuban government. The Cubans want to make it look like a U.S. betrayal. They plan on assassinating the Cuban delegates. And Ryland gets killed in the crossfire—accidentally. Trouble is Ryland has dropped off the radar. His people picked up on disapproval about the meeting. So his security unit took Ryland and hid him away. Nobody knew where, or had any idea when the date of the meeting would get the go-ahead from the senator. But I had an informant close to Ryland's camp. One I kept to myself. Even the Bureau never knew. He managed to get information to me about the date of the meeting. I relayed it to Manolo so he and his group could arrange to be on hand when the senator showed up."

"The meeting's when?" Bolan asked.

"Tomorrow. Ryland will arrive on Soledad Island, just off the Cuban coast, midmorning."

"Manolo turned when you told him what had happened to your money. He figured you might admit your part to the FBI," Bolan said.

Trilling nodded.

"And you went running to Manolo for help," Loomis said. "Not too bright an idea."

"Easy to say that now," Trilling muttered through swollen lips. "I—"

The room's window shattered, glass spraying in glittering arcs. Trilling's head snapped to one side as the first bullet hit. A second followed through. The side of his face blew out in a glistening burst of flesh and bone. The impact pushed Trilling over, the third bullet impacting against the back of his neck, tearing at his spine.

The Executioner felt the warm spray of blood against his face. He heard the solid thump of the bullets as they cleaved into Trilling's flesh, then he was turning, throwing out his arms and planting his hands against Loomis, pushing the cop away from the window. As they fell he heard the heavier thud as more bullets slammed into the wall where they had been standing. The angle of the shots changed, bullets were coming in lower, seeking targets, but Bolan and Loomis were below the trajectory. They lay flat on the floor with the debris from bullet hits in the plaster showering over them.

As suddenly as they started the shots ceased. A momentary calm fell over the room, broken only by the breeze through the shattered window stirring the edges of the blind. A shard of glass dropped from the frame.

The door to the room was thrust open and armed police stood there, staring at the two men on the floor and the broken corpse of Vincent Trilling hanging over the edge of the bed.

Bolan pushed to his feet. He sensed Loomis doing the same.

"Stay clear of the window," Bolan said.

"Call this in," Loomis said to his men. "Start an area search, working back from here. Look for somewhere high up. Get on it."

Loomis brushed plaster dust from his jacket. "That was too damn close to even be funny." He stared at the bloody corpse. "How did they find out he was here so fast?"

"People like Manolo have eyes and ears everywhere. His unlimited wealth means he can buy into anything. Like Trilling here. FBI," Bolan said.

Loomis picked up the unspoken suggestion. For a moment the shadow of anger flashed across his face. Then he regained control.

"I know you're right. We have one of Manolo's snitches in the department. Damn."

The door crashed open again. This time it was uniformed hospital staff, dragging equipment with them.

"No need for any of that," Bolan said. "It's too late." He turned to look out of the window. "Way too late."

CAPSTONE KNEW he'd missed Cooper. His additional shots into Trilling had simply been placed to ensure the man did not survive. By the time he moved the rifle

Cooper had dropped out of sight. Capstone had used up the rest of the magazine, laying down a barrage of shots, hoping to get lucky. He accepted the loss of a second hit. There would be a next time.

He eased away from the firing position, calmly removing the sight from the top of the rifle. He folded the Barrett's stock, opened the case and placed the weapon in its soft sponge base. Then he turned and collected the empty brass shell casings. He dropped them inside the case, closed the lid and locked it. As he stood he picked up the Glock, tucking it behind his belt under his jacket.

Capstone crossed to the ladder and made his way back down to the roof. He took his time, even though he could hear the wail of multiple police sirens. He had expected that every police cruiser in the vicinity would be checking out the area. Capstone didn't panic. He knew he'd be fine as long as he didn't make any stupid moves. He ignored the car. It was rented, and there was nothing to trace it back to him. He had used fake ID to get it. He would walk down and leave by one of the pedestrian exits and lose himself on the crowded streets. Once he was clear of the area he'd grab a cab to get him back to the hotel.

He was one level down when a uniformed security guard appeared. The man was armed, his right hand on the butt of his holstered Beretta.

Capstone stopped, quickly showing a friendly smile. "Hey, you startled me, officer."

The guard looked him over. Capstone sensed tension in the man's attitude. He assumed that news of the hospital shooting has been broadcast on police channels and passed to local security companies.

"You just down from the roof?" the guard asked.

Capstone nodded. The guard was examining him closely.

"Is something wrong, officer?"

The guard picked up chatter from the radio clipped to his belt. He reached out with his left hand to key the button.

"Hey, Gregg, I'm dealing with something. Get back to you."

"Officer, I have a business appointment and I'm already running late," Capstone said.

"Yeah? And do you always go to appointments looking like that?" The guard's tone had sharpened.

"I'm sorry?"

The guard pointed with his left hand. Capstone glanced down. There were dust marks on his pants and jacket.

Capstone swore silently.

A bloody stupid mistake.

He'd forgotten to clean himself off. It was something he would never have forgotten on a preplanned, all-details-covered hit. It was his own fault for accepting a rush job, breaking his own rule and choosing his spot off the cuff.

He'd allowed himself to get a little distracted by Cooper's presence.

He tried to laugh off the guard's interest, at the same time stalling for time. He had to do something fast to get himself out of this spot. Pulling his gun was not realistic. The guard was too close and he had a better chance to draw his own weapon.

"That? It's nothing, officer," he said, keeping his tone light. But he could tell by the guard's expression the man was not backing off.

Capstone took a hesitant step forward. At the same time he used his momentum to swing the gun case, the sharp front edge striking the guard's gun hand, tearing a ragged gash that started to bleed instantly. Capstone kept moving forward, ready to follow with a blow to the guard's throat, but the man recovered faster than he had expected.

The security guard swung his body around, reaching out with his good hand to grab the front of Capstone's jacket and pull him off balance. Capstone felt himself swinging to the side, then gasped as his body slammed into the concrete wall behind him. The guard moved in close, hammering a fist into Capstone's stomach. Capstone dropped the gun case so he had both hands free. As the guard lunged at him, Capstone slammed his clenched fist down hard at the base of the man's skull. The blow stunned the guard for a few seconds, giving Capstone the opportunity to encircle his neck, lock his grip with his other hand and lift the guard off his feet. There was a moment when the man struggled, as if aware what was going to happen, then Capstone heard the dry crunch as the vertebrae just below the skull snapped. He increased the pressure to make sure the injury was severe enough to immobilize the guard. He felt a shudder course through the body before the man became a heavy weight in his hands. Capstone let go and the limp form slumped to the floor.

The hit man quickly retrieved his gun case. He continued down the stairs to street level. As he descended he calmed his breathing, running a hand through his hair to smooth it down. He was angry at what happened but it was done. He had to leave it behind and move on. He pushed through the door and stepped out onto the street, moving at a casual pace as he merged in with the other pedestrians. Out in the open the sound of police sirens was much louder and he spotted a number of cruisers moving along the street.

Capstone walked a block before he hailed a taxi. He slid onto the rear seat, placing his gun case on the floor at his feet. He allowed himself a brief smile as the cab eased into the traffic after he gave the driver his destination. As the vehicle moved off Capstone eased the Glock from his belt and opened the case on the floor. He placed the pistol inside, closed and secured the case, then sat back for the duration of the ride.

When the taxi stopped outside his hotel Capstone reached into his hip pocket and pulled out his wallet. He paid the fare, opened the door and climbed out. Turning to head into the hotel he reached for his room key card in the top pocket of his jacket. His fingers felt the pocket had been torn, leaving one side open. The key card was gone. He remembered instantly the security guard grabbing his jacket during their brief encounter. The card must have slipped out then. Capstone took off his jacket, draping it across his arm and made his way into the hotel. At the desk the clerk nodded in recognition.

"I mislaid my key card. Room 307."

"No problem, Mr. Robbins," the clerk said. "I'll process you another."

Mr. Robbins was booked into one of the most expensive suites in the hotel. He spent freely and handed out good tips. His account was being covered by Santana, Inc., a company that used the hotel for business clients on a regular basis. The desk clerk knew how to treat important clients.

Capstone got the new key card and took the elevator to his room. As he rode up he thought about what to do. Should he remain calm and stay where he was, or check out and find himself a new location? He was still considering his course of action when the car stopped and he made his way to his suite.

It had been a bad day. For the first time in his long career things had not gone according to plan. He corrected himself as he pushed open the door and went into his room.

There hadn't been a fucking plan.

He had allowed himself to be swayed from his usual path simply because of the big bucks Manolo had dangled in front of him. The temptation had been too much for him to ignore. It was enough money to last him the rest of his life. More than enough. It would keep him in luxury. He could retire and lose himself, become someone new. He'd had enough of jetting across the globe, spending long weeks setting up a hit, then making his exit. The thrill of the challenge had waned.

It was time to let go. Manolo's high fee had convinced him. It had seduced him into making a snap decision, stepping over his own demarcation line, and because of that his unblemished record had been tainted.

He placed his gun case on the floor, turned and stood at the window. He had thrown his jacket on the bed and he could see the rip in the top pocket.

It was the simple things in life that could screw you up.

Cooper's image planted itself in his mind. He had almost forgotten about the man in his haste to get away from the killing ground. Now Cooper pushed into his thoughts. Capstone still had that part of his deal to honor and, risky or not, he would take Cooper down before he removed himself from the scene.

He decided it would be wiser to find another place to stay. Capstone called down to the front desk and told them he was going to have to leave due to an unexpected business opportunity that required his presence in Denver. He asked for a taxi to be ordered for a pickup in forty minutes.

He wanted to have a quick shower before he packed. It was part of his usual ritual and he wasn't going to deviate from it anymore. Once he was dressed he threw his torn jacket aside and chose a light brown leather one to replace it. Before he pulled the jacket on he donned a lightweight shoulder rig. He took the Glock from the rifle case and jammed it in the holster.

19

The unmarked police car and an SUV pulled into the semicircular parking area in front of the hotel. As Bolan and Loomis stepped out of their vehicles and headed for the entrance the doorman blocked their way.

"You can't leave—"

Two ID wallets were flashed at him.

"Keep an eye on them," Loomis said.

They went inside, crossing to the desk. The desk manager glanced at them, something in their manner alerting him.

"Can I help you, gentlemen?"

They discreetly displayed their badges.

Bolan placed the hotel key card on the desk.

"Room number? And keep it between us."

The manager slipped the card into the reader.

"Mr. Robbins. 307."

"He in?" Loomis asked.

"Yes. He came back a while ago. He asked for a new card. Said he'd mislaid his."

"Anything else?" Bolan asked.

"He called down twenty minutes ago to say he had to leave. Some urgent business. Asked for a taxi. He wants it twenty minutes from now."

"What do you know about him?" Loomis asked.

"Pleasant enough. Tips well, according to the staff. He has a deluxe suite," the manager said. "That's paid for on an account."

"Who holds the account?" Bolan asked.

The man hesitated. "Look, I don't want to get anyone into trouble, here. I mean…"

"Let me take a guess," Bolan said. "The room is paid for by Raul Manolo."

The manager blinked. "Santana, Inc., in fact. But that is one of Mr. Manolo's businesses."

"Now there's a surprise," Loomis said.

"Here's what I want you to do," Bolan said. "After we go up stop anyone else. Nobody—and I mean nobody—goes up. No exceptions."

At that moment a pair of uniformed cops entered the lobby. They had come in from the back of the hotel so they couldn't be spotted from any of the rooms. Loomis beckoned them over.

"I just told the manager when Cooper and I go upstairs no one follows. I don't care who they are. And no calls from the desk. The phone rings ignore it. You got that, Garrison?"

The cop nodded. "No problem."

"Just remember this guy is good. Don't get careless if he gets by us and shows his face." Loomis drew the other cop to his side. "You're with us, Castle. I want to clear as many rooms near the perp's as we can before we confront him."

The Executioner led the way up the stairs to the third floor. At the landing they assessed the rooms along the corridor.

"Do it quietly. No fuss," Loomis said.

The three men tapped on doors and with each response the occupants were shown badges, the situation explained, and the guests pointed in the direction of the stairs. When all the occupied rooms had been cleared, Castle followed the last hotel guests down to safety in the lobby.

"That went by the book," Loomis observed.

"The next part won't," Bolan replied.

CAPSTONE FINISHED his packing. He picked up the phone to call the desk and check his cab was confirmed. The phone rang continuously. No one picked up. Capstone cut the call, crossed to the window and checked the hotel frontage. He noticed the street in front of the hotel was too quiet. There were no pedestrians and no cars. When he craned his neck to look along the street and through the palms trees edging the sidewalk he caught a glimpse of police cruiser.

"Bloody hell," he said softly.

The bastards had tracked him to the hotel. That missing key card. It had to be.

They must have found it near the dead security guard, and traced him. He glanced at the telephone. That was why there had been no answer. The cops had taken charge. He figured that they would have cleared the rooms on his floor and were most likely waiting outside his door.

Capstone assessed his chances. Slim. He wasn't going to simply walk out of this setup. No bloody way.

He opened the gun case and eased out the Barrett. He snapped in a ten-round magazine and cocked the weapon. He had a number of extra magazines, including some for the Glock, which was snug in its holster.

He turned to the desk and picked up a book of matches bearing the hotel crest, pulled a chair to the spot he wanted and stood on it. Capstone tore off one match and used it to light the others. As the matches flared he reached up and held them beneath the ceiling sprinkler. Nothing happened for long seconds, then the sprinkler sputtered and burst into full flow. The water spray was accompanied by the shrill sound of fire alarms going off.

Ignoring the spray Capstone went to the case and pulled out the smoke canisters. He hefted the Barrett and made for the door. Standing to the side of the door he pulled the pin on one canister and released the lever. Capstone pulled the door open a few inches and tossed the smoking canister into the corridor beyond. He knew that the sprinkler spray would dissipate some of the smoke, but he reasoned there would still be enough to disorientate anyone out there. With the deluge from the sprinklers and the harsh sounds of the fire alarms, there might be enough confusion to give him a fighting chance of evading capture.

He gave the smoke canister a few more seconds, yanked open the door, primed the second canister, lobbed it along the corridor and went out with the rifle up and ready.

"BACK OFF," Bolan said. "Try not to breathe in the smoke."

The coils of thick white smoke issued from the canisters as they rolled along the corridor.

"Either I drown, or die from smoke inhalation," Loomis grumbled, retreating.

The Executioner had pulled back to where the smoke was thinnest, his gaze centered on the door to the target room. The fire alarm and the smoke were nothing but diversions to give their suspect a chance to make a break.

An armed figure burst out of the open doorway and started to lay down rifle fire to the right and left.

The rifle made a big sound and bullets plowed into the corridor walls, blowing out large chunks of plaster. The man swung to the right, aiming in Bolan's direction. Behind the Executioner, at the far end of the corridor, was the emergency door. It opened on a square concrete landing and the steps would allow someone to make a rapid descent from floor to floor. Bolan was sure the hit man would have checked that out on his arrival at the hotel. Despite the smoke he would be able to locate the escape route with ease.

But he had the Executioner between himself and the door.

Bolan had backed along the corridor, managing to stay ahead of the swirling white smoke. He was able to make out the hazy outline of the armed sharpshooter as he headed his way, still firing at random. Bolan dropped to one knee, offering a reduced body mass. He used the muzzle flash from the Barrett to pinpoint his target and raised his Beretta, gripped two-handed as he tracked in.

Coming out of the smoke for a second Capstone saw the crouching figure ahead of him. A tight smile edged his lips. He gripped the rifle and brought the muzzle around and down. One way or the other, if he managed to put Cooper down, perhaps the day wouldn't be a total loss.

The Beretta chugged out a triburst.

Capstone shuddered as the 9 mm slugs struck him in the chest. He set himself against the impact and kept the rifle moving for target acquisition. He pulled the trigger, feeling the big weapon jerk in his grasp. He was sure he had scored a hit. Instead, he saw his slugs plow into the carpeted floor, kicking up shreds of fabric.

Bolan triggered a second burst, the shots turning Capstone around, pushing him against the wall of the corridor. Blood spattered everywhere and his body weight pinned the rifle against the wall. Capstone hung there. He was having trouble breathing. He felt pain in his chest and the coppery taste of blood in his slack mouth. He was on his knees, still gripping the Barrett. Then the wet carpet was against his face.

The Executioner moved to the body and turned the sniper over. He dragged the rifle from the man's grip, looked at the dead face. He recalled an image Kurtzman had displayed during a previous mission.

Victor Capstone. Professional assassin. Ex-SAS. A Brit who had decided to use his sniping skills to take on contract killings.

Loomis was at his side, hair plastered to his skull.

"Cooper, is it always like this with you?"

Bolan shook his head. "Sometimes it gets messy."

"I'll see if I can get them to shut off the damn fire alarm and sprinklers."

Bolan checked Capstone's pockets. He located a cell phone and slipped it out of sight. He might learn something from Capstone's call log.

20

With Loomis handling the follow-up at the hotel, Bolan was able to duck out. He went back to his own hotel and up to his room where he had a shower and changed into dry clothes. He took time to call Stony Man Farm and pass Kurtzman the number of the phone he had taken from Capstone.

"I need to know his recent calls. Who gave him the hospital location."

"Give me an hour and I'll update you."

Bolan reloaded his Beretta, called room service and ordered a meal and coffee.

Kurtzman called back.

"I backtracked on Capstone's cell number. I think the call you were looking for was from a Sgt. Ray Lanning, Miami-Dade P.D. I checked into Lanning's finances. The guy has a nice little nest egg tucked away offshore. I have an address for the man. Has a houseboat moored in a local marina. Lives on board. Unmarried. Guy runs a four-year-old Jeep Cherokee." Kurtzman sighed. "Don't these idiots ever figure even cell phone calls can be traced? Don't they ever think any further than the ends of their noses?"

"Gives me something to move on," Bolan said.

"Good hunting, Striker."

THE EXECUTIONER WAITED until dark before he drove to the marina where Lanning kept his boat. It was a slightly down-market setup. There were no quarter-million-dollar yachts moored. What he saw was more along the lines of floating residences. There were no gleaming white hulls; instead, faded and peeling paint was the norm. He left his SUV in the parking lot above the marina entrance, then walked down the ramp and made his way along the wooden jetty, the decking under his feet rising and falling gently in the swell.

The Last Hand, Lanning's waterborne home, sat high in the water with empty berths on either side. The shallow light from the lamps strung along the jetty showed a boat that needed dry docking and a fresh paint job. The blue-and-white coating looked tired and sun-bleached. Bolan could see light showing through the blinds at the cabin windows. He stepped onto the deck and moved to the sliding access door to the cabin. He could hear the muted drone of a television set.

The door slid open easily. He stepped inside and closed it behind him. Ahead were steps leading down into the main body of the cabin. He could make out the shape of a heavyset man sprawled in a leather recliner, can of beer in one hand, sandwich in the other, as he watched TV. The man wore running shoes, jogging pants and a T-shirt.

The Executioner eased the Beretta 93-R from its holster and moved down the steps. He slipped a small object from his pocket and thumbed a button, holding it in his left hand as he cat-footed across the cabin until he was directly behind the seated man. He pressed the muzzle of the Beretta against the back of the man's broad skull.

"Lanning, Mr. Manolo sends his compliments."

Bolan saw the broad shoulders tense. The head moved slightly to the right and Bolan spotted a 9 mm Beretta sitting on the small side table.

"By the time you drop the beer and reach for it, Lanning, I'll have put three shots into you," he said.

"What the hell is this? A double cross? Manolo got that FBI fuck after I called. I put that guy right on the button for him. I kept my end of the deal."

"Capstone made his hit. Tried for the others in the room but couldn't score with them. Cooper and Loomis are still alive," Bolan said.

"That wasn't my fault. Manolo wanted Trilling dead. He is dead. I earned my money. It's down to Capstone to deal with this guy Cooper. If Loomis gets in the way of a bullet, well, I ain't gonna lose sleep over that."

"Capstone's dead. Cooper got to him first. And Capstone's cell phone had a record of your call on it, Lanning. That's how I found you."

Bolan placed a foot on the side of the recliner and shoved. The chair swiveled, Lanning's arms flinging wide. The can of beer slipped from his grip as the chair swung around. The beefy cop struggled to sit upright. He tossed away the sandwich, gripping the arms of the recliner as he tried to stand. As the chair turned, Lanning came face-to-face with the Executioner as Bolan kicked the side table across the cabin, spinning the cop's Beretta into a corner. Lanning slammed his feet hard on the floor, forcing the recliner to freeze. He stared at Bolan, his heavy features set in a hard scowl. It was only the pistol, fixed solidly on his head, that prevented him from making a reckless move.

Bolan extended his left hand. He showed Lanning what he was holding. It was a digital microrecorder. Bolan switched it off and dropped it back in his pocket.

"That was easier than I expected," he said.

"I thought you were from... Shit, look, just who the fuck are you?" Lanning asked.

"Who I am isn't important. You need to figure out how you can work yourself a deal when they arrest you. In my experience good cops don't like dirty cops. It's going to get rough for you."

"As if I give a shit," Lanning said. "I know my rights. What you just did was illegal."

"Small point, Lanning. I'm not a cop. I work by a different rule book."

Lanning lapsed into a dark silence. His mind was working over his options.

"Damn. I just figured it out. You're Cooper." Lanning grinned. "Manolo wants you so bad it's hurting. He figures you're out to screw up the deal he has going."

"The Ryland operation."

Bolan delivered the words with the conviction of a man who knew exactly what he was talking about. He hoped Lanning understood it that way.

"Hey, I'm not part of that. I just fed Manolo local information."

"In my world, Lanning, you're as guilty as they are. That's how it will read on the indictment. The net catches everybody."

"Wait a minute, Cooper. Nothing's happened yet. Ryland isn't supposed to die until he..." Lanning closed his mouth, staring at Bolan, confusion, then a rising anger, showing on his face. "This is bullshit. I don't say another word until I talk to my lawyer."

"You forgot. This is *my* game, Lanning, and the rules are different. You have no rights. Forget lawyers. You're in the twilight world. One call and you vanish. No one will ever know what happened to you. Try me, tough guy."

Bolan took out his phone and tapped in a number. When his call was picked up he spoke quickly.

"Ray Lanning's boat. Know where it is? I need transport. Now."

"Who the fuck was that?" Lanning asked.

"Your escort to a new home. Take a last look around. No more boat, Lanning. No more anything."

Lanning stared into those cold blue eyes. He knew, without a shadow of a doubt, that this man meant every word he said.

"How do we make a deal?" he asked.

The Executioner backed across the cabin, giving himself distance from Lanning. He didn't want to allow the cop any chance to make a grab for his gun.

"I'm prepared to listen if you want to tell me something."

"I can give you Cassidy. And the military guy, Kirby," Lanning said.

GARY LOOMIS ARRIVED twenty minutes later. He slid open the cabin door and stepped inside, followed by a pair of uniforms. He surveyed the scene.

"Somebody better tell me what the hell is going on here," he demanded.

Bolan took out the microrecorder and worked the switches. He held it up so they could all hear what Lanning had said. Bolan could see Loomis getting angrier as the accusatory words filled the cabin. When the recording had finished Bolan passed the recorder to the cop.

Lanning stayed silent.

"He's all yours. He wants to hear his rights. Keeps asking for his lawyer. Believes it should all be done by the book," Bolan said.

Loomis told his officers to cuff Lanning and put him in their cruiser. He went and picked up Lanning's pistol, and the uniforms hustled Lanning out of the cabin. As he passed Bolan the dirty cop turned.

"You fucking tricked me," he said.

Bolan nodded. "It was so easy," he said.

"Guys, take it easy with your prisoner. I wouldn't want him bumping his head on the way up that jetty," Loomis said.

Loomis turned his attention to Bolan.

"How'd you find him, Cooper?"

"We got lucky."

"Yeah. I could use some of your *luck*."

"There's something I have to follow up," Bolan said. "Then I might call on you for help."

"All you have to do is ask," Loomis said.

THE HOTEL WHERE Douglas Kirby was staying was off the main drag, set back from the road. Even at night the shabbiness showed. The place had seen better days. Bolan headed for the entrance. He was almost there when he halted midstride. Passing the parking lot he recognized a vehicle he had seen before. He crossed to check it out more closely, laying a hand on the hood. Warmth from the engine still remained.

Bolan picked up speed, pushing in through the main door. The lobby was dimly lit. The front desk was deserted. The computer was sitting on the counter. Bolan quickly searched the guest registry. Kirby's name was there. He had booked in two days earlier.

Bolan headed for the stairs and ran up to the next floor.

He took the corridor to his left, counting off the doors. Kirby's was midway along. He slid the Beretta from the shoulder holster as he approached. Raised voices could be heard coming from inside the room. Bolan tried the handle. The door was locked.

"No, damn you. Get the hell out, Cassidy."

The Executioner raised his foot and slammed it against the panel just below the handle. The door crashed against the inner wall, splintering.

Kirby stared at him over Brett Cassidy's shoulder. His face was glistening with sweat, blood running from the corner of his mouth.

"Get him out of here," he shouted. "The bastard is crazy. He's going to kill me."

Cassidy hit Kirby across the side of the head with the barrel of the heavy auto pistol he held. He lunged forward and caught hold of Kirby's shirtfront, pulling the man around to cover himself, the muzzle of his pistol pressed against Kirby's cheek. As he looked at the intruder he recognized Bolan.

"Hey, Cooper. Haven't seen you for a while. What the hell happened? You look a mess."

"Ask your buddy Manolo. He can tell you."

"You lost me there, Coop. I'm after Manolo. Just like you."

"No. You're working with him. Same as Kirby. Only Manolo wants him out of the picture now he's no use any longer."

"Coop, this crazy."

"I saw you, Cassidy. The night they jumped me at my motel. When they drugged me and took me to Colombia. You were with Santiago."

"You're crazy! I don't know what you're talking about," Cassidy said desperately.

"I know what I saw. My way is faster, Cassidy," the Executioner said.

The ATF agent frowned and pointed his pistol at Bolan. "What way?"

Bolan didn't answer. He triggered a three-round burst that ripped through Cassidy's right elbow where it jutted out beyond Kirby's body. Cassidy's pistol dropped from his hand and he stumbled back from Kirby. The ATF man made a grab for the fallen pistol, just reaching the butt, when the Executioner sent a second triburst into the side of his head, shattering his skull.

Kirby turned and ran into the bathroom.

"Leave the door open," Bolan said.

He could see Kirby wet a towel and dab at the bleeding gash in his head.

"Manolo wants you dead, too," the army major said as he stepped back into the room.

"That's the only thing we have in common, then, Kirby."

Kirby leaned against the wall. He was a man with nothing left in him. Any fight he had was gone.

"What now?"

"I make a call. After that you're on your own." Bolan called Hal Brognola and told him what had happened. "Have Kirby picked up by the local force. Make it fast. I can't wait around here too long. I have to be somewhere."

"You okay, Striker? Maybe you should—"

"I'm fine," he said and ended the call.

Bolan heard the approaching police cruisers within minutes. He stayed at the door of the room as uniformed cops came up the stairs. He had his ID ready when they came into the room.

"He needs medical attention," Bolan said, indicating Kirby. He turned to leave the room. "I'll give your best to Manolo when I see him," he said to Kirby.

"He's going to kill you," Kirby said.

"That isn't going to happen," Bolan said. "Neither is *Paso Tresero*."

21

Loomis checked the chart Bolan had spread out.

"Soledad Island. It's small. Seven miles off Cuba," Bolan said. "Before the revolution it belonged to a wealthy family. There's a large hacienda there. The government took it over and it's used for official purposes now. Ideal for whatever Manolo has planned. And it's happening tomorrow. We have no way of contacting Ryland, so the only thing is to be there."

"My turn," Loomis said, pointing out the single-engine Cessna seaplane moored at the police jetty. "Belonged to a Miami drug trafficker. He killed an FBI agent when they went to arrest him. He's doing life, so he won't be needing it. It was seized along with his other property when the verdict came in. Seems a shame to let it stand idle."

Bolan glanced across at the cop. "Gary, this is no picnic I'm heading for. You've met the kind of people involved. It could get nasty."

"Working Miami-Dade is no soft touch, Cooper. I'm a big boy. Don't worry about me. I want to help. Simple as that." Loomis paused. "You did my department a big favor when you pulled Lanning into the light. It's hard enough working the job without having one of your own screwing you. MDPD owes you, Cooper, and we pay our debts."

"How soon can you have that plane ready to go?"

"An hour soon enough?"

"It will have to be."

Loomis nodded. "Meet you here at eleven."

BOLAN DROVE BACK to his hotel. In his room he checked over his arsenal, loading up and adding extra magazines to his harness rig. A compact transceiver was included. He donned his blacksuit and combat boots. The weaponry and holsters went into a long black bag. A compact set of binoculars, housed in a small zipped case, looped on his belt. He pocketed a bunch of plastic restraints, and placed all his other personal items in his travel bag, locked it and stowed it in the closet. He called the desk, informing them he wanted no disturbances for the night. With that done he slipped on a leather jacket, picked up his war bag and left. He zipped the room key card in a jacket pocket, and took an elevator down to the basement garage.

It took him just over fifteen minutes to make it back to the small dock where Loomis had the Cessna warmed up and ready to go. Bolan crossed the dock. Behind him the lights of Miami blazed. The air was warm, almost sullen. Loomis followed Bolan into the plane.

He watched as Bolan transferred his ordnance from the carryall into a waterproof bag. He didn't fail to notice the range of weapons. Bolan closed the zip and checked that the seal was intact before he stowed the bag behind the seat.

"Cooper, that's serious ordnance you're hauling."

"Manolo isn't going to welcome me with a bunch of flowers."

Loomis secured the cabin hatch. "Not when he sees that hardware."

Bolan dropped into the copilot's seat as Loomis taxied the Cessna over the water, away from the dock. He held up a strip of paper showing the frequency the transceiver was set to. Loomis took the slip and put it away.

"I give you a call, come and get me," Bolan said.

"You got it."

Once they were airborne Loomis set the course. He glanced at his watch. Ahead, the night sky was gathering dark clouds.

"Forecast warned there might be some rain up ahead," he said.

"It should give us some cover when we get near," Bolan replied. "Could help me on the ground."

Loomis reached behind him and produced a canvas bag. He took out a steel flask. "Coffee," he said. "I guessed you wouldn't have had much chance to get any."

Bolan opened the flask. He poured black coffee into a mug Loomis produced, then into his own. The coffee tasted good.

The Cessna pushed south, the sky filling with heavy clouds ahead.

"This bunch Manolo is heading. They really believe Ryland is that much of a threat?" Loomis asked.

"Anything likely to interfere with the status quo is a threat. Kickbacks, black-market trading—it's bringing in big money. Manolo has his drug business up and running, and his connections in Cuba allow him a solid distribution base to operate from. The Cuban minister Perez is representing others in the government, as well as himself. They don't want any kind of change in policy. The Communist power base has to keep control. If it topples they all lose the benefits of the regime. And if they implicate the U.S. making a hard strike at the Cuban representatives, it adds fuel to their argument that the regime needs to stay firm."

"So they keep the country under their heel. Make the Cuban people toe the line just so they can keep living the high life."

"Survival for the top men running a crumbling dictatorship. As long as they deny the people any strength they keep things as they are. It's an old story, Gary. And painting the U.S. as the capitalist devil is par for the course."

"Cooper, just make sure you kick some serious butt down there."

Thirty minutes out from the target the rain swept in.

A fierce squall gripped the Cessna and shook it, the rain pounding the aircraft. Loomis switched on the wipers. They swept back and forth, struggling to clear the screen. Bolan watched the Miami cop, impressed by his handling of the situation. Loomis had a natural ability. His coordination kept them on course, despite a few dips and lurches caused by the rough spots they flew into. The rain stayed with them all the way. Despite the conditions Loomis brought the Cessna down only a few degrees away from the map coordinates. Once he coasted the seaplane into the small bay the sea swell subsided enough that he was able to get close to shore. He used the twin lights mounted under the wings to guide the aircraft in.

"Sorry I can't drop you any closer, Cooper."

"This is fine," Bolan said. "You sure about staying around?"

"Hey, let me tell you about the days I've spent on stakeouts. Stuck in the same damn car until you feel like you're part of the seat."

"Sounds cozy."

"Not the word I would choose."

Bolan cracked the hatch, feeling the rain wet his face. He swung the sealed bag holding his weapons over his back, securing the straps, then stepped out onto the pontoon. He raised a quick hand to Loomis, closed the hatch and let himself down into the water, pushing away from the Cessna toward the shore.

He stepped out of the water minutes later, oblivious to the rain still dropping from the black sky. He found a shallow cave just up from the beach. It allowed him to lay his sealed bag beside him while he unzipped one of his blacksuit pockets and slid out the small laminated map of the island. He grabbed a small waterproof penlight and found his current position, then followed the contours of the map until he located the target area.

If he made good time he could be at the hacienda by dawn. Then he'd find himself a secure spot and run his recon as soon as it got light. He was assuming that Manolo would have some of his own people working security, and that they would not reveal themselves in case they caused too much suspicion when Ryland's team arrived with the senator. Official security, provided by the Cubans, was one thing. A secondary force, well armed and prowling the immediate area, might plant seeds of doubt, and Ryland's security team might play safe and call off the meeting. Manolo had to get Ryland on the ground and within his grasp before he made his move.

If that meant Manolo had his own people roving the area at a distance it would give the Executioner the opportunity to whittle them down, out of sight of the main building.

Manolo's people had tortured and killed Maggie Connor. They had slaughtered her house staff. Bolan had seen the results of their handiwork, and faced their unrelenting hostility, and those images would be on his mind when he came face-to-face with the hired butchers.

Bolan fixed his route in his mind. He stowed the small map away and turned to his sealed bag. Opening it, he removed his equipment and laid it out, checking that everything was dry. Satisfied he pulled on the combat harness and the shoulder rig for the Beretta. He belted on the holstered Desert Eagle and a sheathed knife. Then he checked both pistols and the Uzi, ensuring the actions were operating and the loaded magazines were sound. He reloaded and pushed the first rounds into the breeches. At the bottom of his waterproof bag he found the black baseball cap he'd included and pulled it on. The Uzi was suspended by its nylon strap around his neck and across his torso.

His final act was to check the transceiver.

Loomis responded immediately.

"You're not going to tell me it's done already?"

"Equipment check is all, Gary."

"You came through fine."

"You shouldn't hear from me again until I need a ride."

"Hey, watch yourself, Cooper."

"Will do."

Bolan clicked off the connection and secured the transceiver.

Easing from the shelter Bolan picked up his trail and moved off, his steady pace taking him toward Manolo's Cuban base of operations.

22

The rain faded as the first flickers of dawn paled the sky. Emerging from heavy undergrowth the Executioner crouched in the shadows, took out his binoculars and made his first scan of the hacienda. From his vantage point he was able to look down on the well-established house and grounds, all contained inside an encircling wall. The size of the house was impressive. It stood on two levels, with wide patios and enclosed courtyards. Stone steps led to the various levels, covered verandas and terraces. The building had white walls and a terracotta roof. There was a large swimming pool at the back, surrounded by wide lawns and deep flower beds. Where the paved driveway ended at the imposing frontage of the house a number of cars were in evidence. The span of the enclosed grounds was large enough for a helipad. The south side of the house was close to the water, with a curving white beach and a modern jetty that had a number of small motor launches moored alongside.

As the light became stronger Bolan used the binoculars to run a full visual scan of the entire area. He saw no movement around the house, or on the grounds, but when he extended his range he picked up four armed men on loose patrols at different points around the perimeter walls. He focused on one. The man was lean, wearing a long raincoat and a baseball cap. He carried a Franchi-SPAS combat shotgun that dangled off his left shoulder from a sling. He moved slowly, dragging his feet, sucking on a thick cigar. A check of the other patrollers confirmed for Bolan that these were Manolo's hired guns. There was nothing in their manner to suggest military or security training. He didn't want these men wandering around beyond his immediate control once he got closer to the hacienda.

He put the binoculars away and glanced skyward. Another half hour would see full light.

He negotiated the uneven slope that took him in the direction of the closest guard. He kept to cover as much as he could while holding the guard in his sight. He moved along a path that would eventually intersect with that of the patrolling man.

With only yards to go Bolan stayed low, using the lush vegetation to hide as the guard approached. The gunman wasn't very careful. If he had been on patrol for a few hours his concentration had most likely faded to its lowest point.

Bolan let the man walk past him, then rose, silent and smooth, stepping in close and grabbing him in a headlock. He applied a choke hold, shutting off the blood supply to the man's brain. The guard struggled frantically, his movements slowing until he was dead weight. Bolan secured the unconscious guard's wrists and ankles with plastic restraints. He used his knife to cut a long strip from the man's coat, using it to gag the man, then dragged him out of sight under thick bushes.

Bolan snatched up the SPAS shotgun. He faded into the background foliage and circled around the estate until he spotted another guard. Emerging from cover on the man's left side the Executioner slammed the butt of the shotgun into his ribs, followed by another one that connected with the jaw. The guard grunted, blood spraying from his mouth, as he stumbled to his knees. Before he had any chance to react Bolan slammed the shotgun down across the back of his skull, pitching the man facedown and unconscious on the rain-soaked ground. Bolan disarmed him, bound his ankles and wrists, then repeated the operation with the knife. He tied the gag tight, hauled the inert form out of sight and moved on to locate guard number three.

Minutes later there was only one guard to be dealt with. He sighted his quarry and closed in to make his move.

In the final moment before Bolan struck, the guard turned his head, locked eyes with his attacker and evaded Bolan's first strike with surprising agility. He was tall, wide shouldered, his arms long and powerful as they swept up and brushed aside the Executioner as easily as he might have warded off a child. Bolan went down, the impact reduced by the soft, waterlogged ground. He rolled onto his back, reluctant to use his weapon because of the noise any shot might create. His opponent had no such notion, grabbing for the submachine gun swinging from his shoulder.

Bolan saw this slight delay as his only chance. He didn't waste time trying to climb to his feet, aware that such an action would give his opponent ample time to bring his own weapon into play. Bolan simply brought his legs around in a powerful sweep that took the guard's feet from under him. He landed on his back, hard, unable to cushion his fall. Before he was able to recover,

Bolan had rolled to a crouch, lashing out with his right leg, the toe of his boot slamming into the man's neck and crushing everything in its path. The guard's eyes widened in alarm as he found he was unable to breath. He clutched at his throat, head rolling from side to side, and quickly succumbed to his injuries.

On his knees Bolan took a moment to catch his breath after the short but brutal engagement. He checked his equipment. Nothing had been damaged.

He stood upright, moving quickly as he took his final approach to the estate.

SENATOR PAUL RYLAND finished dressing, went downstairs and had his customary two cups of coffee and a slice of rye toast while he read the morning newspaper. If he had been anything less than the optimist he was, the usual headlines proclaiming doom and disaster might have plunged him into despair. Ryland folded the newspaper and pushed it aside.

His chief minder, Agent Steve Cameron, entered the room.

Cameron, six-two and wide shouldered, had the build of a quarterback. He was quick, agile and seemed to have all-round vision. Always immaculately dressed he presented a figure of authority.

"Is everything ready?" Ryland asked.

"We leave in five, sir. Transport at the door, direct run to the liftoff point. Flight shouldn't take more than an hour and a half." Cameron paused. "That's if you still insist on doing this."

"Damn it, Steve, I thought we'd finished with this conversation."

"I wouldn't be doing my job if I didn't try to persuade you to give it up."

"Because you don't trust Perez."

"That and the fact we've had hints this meeting might go wrong."

"That's why we've kept it under wraps. Closed all communications as to when and where. Isolated me here in this rented place. No one knows where we are. No one can contact us. Jesus, Steve, I feel like a prisoner in solitary."

"Necessary precautions, Senator. We leave for the meet in total secrecy. Fly out from a place of my choosing. By the time we get there no one will even know you left the mainland."

Ryland picked up his briefcase and went through the documents inside. He settled the papers, closed and locked the case again.

"Okay, Steve," he said, "I'm all yours."

Cameron nodded. He raised his hand and spoke into the microphone that jutted from the cuff of his shirt. He waited until he had received the all clear from his two other agents.

"Senator, we're good to go."

Ryland followed him outside, straight to the black car waiting for them, motor gently idling. The point man got in beside the driver, Cameron in the rear with Ryland. The whole move from house to vehicle was done smoothly, without pause, and Ryland had barely settled in his seat before they drove off. A second vehicle, an identical model, pulled in behind to shadow Ryland's.

"Nicely done, Steve."

Cameron gave one of his rare smiles. "We were up all night practicing, Senator," he said. "Right, guys?"

"Right, Agent Cameron," the point man said.

"You have them well trained, Steve."

A cell phone trilled and the agent in the front seat picked up and listened.

"Chopper is warmed up and ready to lift off," he said.

The car weaved its way steadily through the morning traffic, the tail car never losing its position behind them. Ryland sat back, content to let his escort do its job. In the two years Cameron and his team had been providing security for him there had never been a hint of a problem. It spoke well of their professionalism.

Twenty minutes later they pulled off the highway and passed through the gate that gave access to the small, private airstrip that had been quietly vetted by Cameron's team. The owner had not been consulted until the day before, his cooperation assured when the security team had descended on the strip and maintained their presence through the night. Once the helicopter took off, the team would climb into their vehicles and leave, job done and the senator safely on his way.

The helicopter sat in isolation, rotors turning slowly. The vehicle drove as close as it could so Ryland was able to walk quickly to the open hatch and climb inside. He was escorted by Cameron and three of his men. The moment the hatch closed the pilot increased power and lifted off quickly, swinging the chopper in a tight curve that put it on a direct course for Ryland's rendezvous.

CROUCHING ON A SLIGHT rise overlooking the estate Bolan took out his binoculars and focused in on the group standing near the helipad. He recognized Raul Manolo even before he used the binoculars. Dressed in light, casual slacks and a colored shirt, Manolo was easy to spot. Chico Delgado was next to him. Just behind Manolo were a trio of figures. Bodyguards by their size and stance.

Just ahead of Manolo was a man Bolan couldn't place until he centered the binoculars on him. He flipped through the images stored in his head. Images he had first seen back at Stony Man Farm when Kurtzman had shown him photographs taken by Maggie Connor.

It was Santos Perez. The Cuban government minister.

Perez was smartly dressed in a suit and tie. He kept glancing skyward. When Bolan focused in on the man's fleshy face he detected a slight nervous expression. Perez checked his watch, turning to speak to Manolo, who patted his arm in a calming gesture. Again Perez raised his eyes to the sky.

Bolan understood.

Minister Santos Perez, the official Cuban representative, was on hand to welcome Senator Ryland to the hacienda. The trusted face there to assure Ryland everything was fine. To make sure that Ryland's own security escort was put at ease, taking them into a safety zone before the trap was sprung.

With Ryland his captive, Manolo could set his charade into motion. He'd bring on his "American" strike force to act out their deadly hit against the meeting, and during the firefight Ryland would become an unfortunate victim. The peace accord would end in a bloody confrontation, the Cuban representatives killed and doubters in Havana proved correct. America was not to be trusted. It would appear the Americans had orchestrated the strike in order to shatter the possibility of cooperation between the two countries. The Marxist cadre would be strengthened and Manolo's consortium would see their illegal activities become even more strongly entrenched.

Perez suddenly pointed up. A rapidly expanding speck approached the location. Ryland's helicopter. Below, Manolo waved his people away. The area was cleared, leaving only Perez and the trio of security men flanking him. Like Perez, they were dressed in conservative suits and ties. Honey baiting the trap.

The chopper swung in over the estate, dropping lower as it hovered above the helipad. Perez stepped forward a few feet, then waited. The chopper sank toward the ground.

The Executioner headed for the area. He brought the SPAS into play as a simple thought came into his mind. He had to warn Ryland's people there was a problem. To do that he had to attract their attention before his chance slipped away.

The noise of the SPAS being discharged would do it. Perez and his escort would react, too. The combination would be enough to alert Ryland's team. Standing orders in such a situation would be to remove their principal from the area. Nothing else mattered. Ryland would be flown clear of the landing site, maybe even returned directly to the safety of the mainland. The meeting would be declared compromised. There would be a lot of ruffled feathers, but at least Ryland would have been removed to home ground.

The helicopter was no more than a couple of feet from touchdown as Bolan raised the SPAS.

He felt the cold ring of metal press into the back of

his neck. Felt the brutal thrust of a second weapon against his ribs.

A hand snatched the shotgun from his grasp.

"No, I do not think that would be a good idea."

Something hard struck Bolan across the back of his skull. The blow dropped him to his knees and he heard someone laugh. Hands gripped his arms to drag him upright. Bolan focused his eyes. He saw the helicopter land. The cabin door opened and the passengers stepped out. Perez was standing in front of the group, one hand extended to Senator Ryland.

Too late, Bolan thought. I was too damn late.

He saw the distant group walking away from the helicopter toward the house.

As his captors pulled him to his feet Bolan took an observant glance to his left and right. Just the single pair. No others.

Bolan felt hands touching him, seeking to strip away his weapons and leave him defenseless. The sensation triggered his response and when he moved he did so with such speed that his captors had no chance.

The Executioner turned to his left, the edge of his hand sweeping around in a bone-shattering strike for the throat of the man there. The recipient felt only the deep impact of the blow as his flesh caved in. The collapse of his air passages left him struggling for the breath that was never going happen again. He was too involved in trying to regain control that he offered no resistance when Bolan drove his booted foot against his right knee, crushing the bone and dropping him to the ground.

The flurry of movement on his right only guided Bolan to his second target. The startled man was trying to level his weapon. Bolan hit him with a looping left that slammed against an exposed jaw. The powerful blow took the jaw out of its socket, the lower half of the man's face taking on a skewed look. As he continued his movement Bolan snaked his right arm around the man's neck. He pulled hard enough so that the guard's feet left the ground. He maintained his hold until he heard the soft snap of vertebrae. The man shuddered, then stilled. Bolan let go and the body dropped facedown.

He picked up the discarded shotgun. Checking out the grounds he saw Ryland being escorted inside the house.

The man was still alive.

But for how long?

He cut off in the direction of the residence, his first hurdle the encircling wall. Beyond that he would face Manolo's force of armed men. He had no idea how strong that force was. He reached the wall and searched for a way in, spotting a side gate some yards to his right.

The Executioner accepted the challenge without pause.

23

The Executioner turned in the direction he had seen Senator Ryland and company move.

He was closing in on the hacienda when he caught movement out the corner of his eye. An armed figure was emerging from heavy foliage, a submachine gun in his hands. A second man was on his heels, already talking into his transceiver. The first man swung the weapon into firing position, the muzzle angling in Bolan's direction, and the Executioner knew it was going down *now*.

Bolan turned, the SPAS swinging with him. The weapon was set for semiautomatic, the first shell already loaded. As the muzzle tracked in he eased the trigger back, feeling the heavy shotgun recoil as it blew its 12-gauge shot at the oncoming gunner. The range was close enough to keep the pattern tight, and the gunner took the full brunt of the blast in his torso. The stricken man was propelled back in a welter of bloody tissue, the suddenness of the act forcing his partner to sidestep, already triggering his own weapon in a desperate attempt to put Bolan down. His change of direction, slight as it was, gave Bolan a microsecond of advantage and he used it well, hitting the trigger again and delivering a solid shot into the gunner's shoulder. The man fell to the ground, writhing in agony before the surge of pain sucked him into unconsciousness.

The shots broke the silence surrounding the house, alerting Manolo's force. The Executioner knew there was little time for anything except a head-on attack.

He turned at an angle, making for the open access to the rear of the house.

He was almost there when a figure dressed in a casual shirt and pants appeared through an open arch. He was carrying a Heckler & Koch MP-5 and he opened fire the moment he set eyes on the intruder. The spray of 9 mm slugs ripped into the turf under Bolan's feet as he veered to one side, shouldering his shotgun and returning fire. The blast from the SPAS pitted the stone wall close to the other man, peppering the side of his face with hot flecks. The gunman gasped and shook his head. That response allowed Bolan to put his next shot into the man's chest. The man stumbled and fell backward, his MP-5 clattering across the patio.

Stepping over the prone body Bolan cut through a flower bed and flattened himself against the wall by the open door. As he braced himself he heard the sound of rushing footsteps, angry voices cursing in Spanish. Then a dark shape burst through the door, pausing to check for signs of the intruder, his weapon gripped tight as he searched the area. As the excited man tried to take aim, Bolan remained calm. He half turned, carefully directing the muzzle of the shotgun and pulling the trigger. The man remained standing for a few seconds, even taking a hesitant step, before his body shut down and he collapsed.

The Executioner went through the door, the SPAS covering the way ahead. He heard an intake of breath and sensed a dark shape looming on his left. Bolan pulled the shotgun into a defensive position as a tall, heavy man lunged at him. A keen-bladed machete burned the air as it slashed at Bolan. The blade hit the SPAS, the impact almost knocking the weapon from Bolan's hands. He managed to retain his grip on the weapon as he pulled away from his opponent, needing a second or two to set himself. Bolan reacted to the machete strike, ducking beneath the follow-up stroke. The blade hissed as it cut the air just above Bolan's head. The Executioner drove himself forward, slamming a shoulder into his attacker's stomach. The guard groaned, falling back, pain etched across his face. Bolan straightened, slamming the SPAS across the side of the man's face. The blow snapped his head back with a sodden crunch.

Bolan heard the sound of weapons being cocked. He picked up the movement as reinforcements jostled through the gap just ahead. He flattened against the wall to the left of the opening, waiting as two armed men rushed through, pausing when they saw one of their own sprawled in a bloody pool on the ground. Bolan had his window of opportunity and he took it, cutting loose with the shotgun. He triggered three shots, taking down the pair before they shot him.

Throwing down the shotgun, Bolan brought the Uzi into play as he moved into the hacienda, determined to locate Ryland and his team.

He hoped he wasn't too late.

PAUL RYLAND WOULD HAVE been the first to admit to a degree of bewilderment at the sudden turn of events.

What had begun as a hopeful meeting between like-minded people turned into a nightmare. The sudden appearance of Raul Manolo, with his threats and Ryland's planned demise, had left the senator dismayed. But Ryland was no naive politician. He understood the brutality of men like Manolo and that killing him and anyone else involved in the peace accord would mean nothing to Raul Manolo.

Along with his security team Ryland was held under the guns of Manolo's fake military. There was nothing any of them could do. Glancing across at Cameron, Ryland could see the man's anguish. Cameron would blame himself for what had happened. Ryland knew the man well enough to understand his feelings. Cameron would be seething inside, embarrassed at allowing his charge to be taken from him at gunpoint. What would hurt more was that Cameron and his team had been helpless, unable to do a thing to protect Ryland. In his world Cameron should have taken on the hostiles and fought back. Cameron would be seeing the incident as a complete betrayal of his responsibility.

"Steve," Ryland said, catching the man's attention.

"No talking!" one of the gunmen said.

Ryland turned to face the man.

"Or what?" he asked, his own frustration rising in a flash of defiance. "You going to shoot me? Without getting the go-ahead from your boss? I don't think so. It might screw up his plans."

The gunman moved forward, raising his weapon. Behind him one of the others reached out and grabbed his arm.

"Back off," he said. "Manolo will tear off your head if you fuck up."

The gunman relented grudgingly. He jabbed a finger in Ryland's direction. "Your time's coming."

"Senator, don't push him," Cameron said.

Ryland turned back to his security chief. He placed a hand on Cameron's broad shoulder.

"I'm sorry about this, Steve. I played right into Manolo's hands. Had my eye on coming out of this meeting with success written across my chest. I really got this wrong."

"You did it by the book, Senator. The idea was sound. How were we to know Manolo was going to hijack the meeting for his own agenda?"

The distant boom of a shotgun reached them followed by the crackle of automatic fire.

"What the hell is that?"

The man who had threatened Ryland moved toward the door.

"We need to find out what's happening out there."

"Hey, we were told to stay here," one of the other guards said.

"Fuck that. Maybe we've been compromised. You two, come with me. The rest of you stay with the pigeons," he said, gesturing to the remaining two.

They moved to the door. As it opened, the shotgun fired again, the sound coming from the rear of the hacienda.

"Let's move."

THE EXECUTIONER HIT the passage on the run. The shotgun blasts would have alerted everyone inside the house. He knew he could expect a response at any moment.

He was prepared for it.

Halfway along the passage he was confronted by three armed men as they came out of a door, dressed in U.S. military gear and carrying Benelli M4 rifles. He could tell instantly that these men were not real soldiers. Their lack of discipline exposed their charade. They opened fire the moment their eyes locked onto Bolan's black-clad figure, the passage echoing to the bursts of automatic fire.

Bolan had dropped, hitting the tiled floor and rolling to one side. The gunfire sent slugs burning the length of the passage. Skidding to a halt the soldiers altered their aim seconds behind Bolan.

The Uzi chattered sharply as Bolan locked in on the closest gunman and hit him with a short burst to the torso. As the fatally hit man went down Bolan changed position and raked the other two with more 9 mm fire, his bursts hitting them in the lower torsos and legs. The hot burn of the slugs knocked the pair off balance and as they went down Bolan hit them again, his hard fire ripping into their chests. The bloodied figures hit the floor, weapons forgotten as their worlds turned into a pain-filled hell. Pushing to his feet and slinging the Uzi by its strap Bolan snatched up one of the dropped M4s.

He covered the distance to the door the three men had exited and pressed up against the wall. The door was partially open and he picked up the murmur of voices inside.

"Go and check. I'll keep them covered," someone said in Spanish.

The sound of boots moving across the room warned Bolan. He stayed where he was, the M4 braced across his chest. The door was pulled wide and an armed figure came into view. His head was still turning in Bolan's direction when the M4 swept around and cracked against his jaw. The man grunted, stunned. Bolan stepped in front of him, pushing against the man's chest and backpedaling him into the room. Over the man's shoulder Bolan saw a lone, armed man standing watch over Paul Ryland and his people.

The second gunman spotted Bolan as he shouldered aside the man he had used for cover, knocking him to the floor. He also saw the Executioner's M4 as it lined up and crackled briefly, sending a trio of bullets into his head. The man stumbled back, hitting the wall and leaving a red smear as he slid to the floor.

"Son of a bitch…!"

The shout came from the surviving gunman. He scrabbled for the M4 he had dropped.

Across the room Steve Cameron had crouched, snatching up the weapon of the man who'd been shot. The security man swung the rifle around and triggered a burst that put Bolan's attacker down hard.

"At least I got that right," Cameron growled. He stared at Bolan. "And who the hell are you?"

"I'm the one who's about to put an end to this," the Executioner said.

He handed over his M4 to one of the other American security agents.

"I guess I owe you some thanks," Ryland said. "And I guess I should have listened to your warnings, Steve."

"Kiss and make up later," Bolan said. "Out the door.

Turn left. Follow through and it should take you out near your helicopter."

Ryland was about to say something. All he got was the black-clad man's back as Bolan turned and exited the room.

24

Raul Manolo grabbed his Glock pistol and snapped back the slide.

"What's happening?" Luis Costa asked.

They heard the sound of more gunshots.

"It's him," Manolo said.

He crossed to the computer that controlled the hacienda's security cameras and began to press some keys. The row of monitors came to life, each displaying a different location both inside and outside of the house.

Moving to stand behind his employer Costa himself was the first to spot the black-clad figure moving purposely along one of the passages. "There he is," he said pointing at a monitor.

"That man is haunting me," Manolo said. "Every time I turn around he's there. It's like a curse."

One of the screens showed Ryland and his security team crossing an exterior patio. The American bodyguards were armed again. Manolo slammed his fist on the desk.

"Raul, what do we do? Ryland is still alive. Perez will be panicking if he heard the shooting," Costa said.

Manolo regained a degree of control. "Call the boat. Tell Quintero to ready it for leaving."

"But—"

"Luis, we have lost. We can't pull it off now. So we

cut our losses and get out of here. I have no intention of getting myself killed over this."

Costa nodded. He picked up the phone and tapped in a number. He relayed Manolo's orders to *La Perla*'s captain.

Pulling a transceiver from his pocket Manolo snapped out instructions to his remaining people.

"Find that American, Cooper. It's open season. I'll pay a million dollars to the man who brings me his head." He threw the transceiver across the room. "Let's go home, Luis." He glanced across the room at Delgado. "You wanted to be a full partner, Chico. Here's your chance. Take out that fancy gun you carry and be ready to use it."

The men left the room. On one of the monitors the image of the grim, blacksuited figure dominated the screen as the Executioner moved through the property.

DIRECTLY AHEAD OF HIM a wood-framed door loomed. Bolan raised a hard boot to kick it open, then ducked low as he emerged into a wide, open courtyard.

Raised voices told him his presence had been acknowledged. He knew any opportunity for stealth had been purged by his active fire, so he hit the open courtyard on full alert. Eyes sweeping the area he spotted a pair of armed men in civilian clothing racing in his direction. Bolan went down on his knees, sliding across the smooth pavement to come up hard at the base of the large ornamental fountain in the center of the courtyard. He heard one of the men shout a warning. The courtyard echoed to the savage rattle as the advancing pair opened fire. Double streams of bullets hammered at the fountain, blowing shards of stone from the sculpture.

The Executioner felt the chips rain across his back.

He worked his way around the circular base of the fountain, leaning around the wide curve of stone, and saw one of the pair already moving in that direction. Bolan swept the M4 around and hit the man midthigh with a sustained burst, dumping him, screaming, on the ground. The gunman's weapon spilled from his hands as he squirmed in agony. Bolan triggered the M4 again and put the man out of his misery. He heard the other man shout in dismay at the demise of his partner. The man swung around the fountain, eyes lowered as he sought out Bolan. The Executioner pushed to his feet and brought his rifle on target, aiming through the clear water splashing down from the head of the fountain. Bolan hit the trigger and sent a heavy burst into the gunner's chest, blowing him backward. The man didn't make a sound as he landed hard, his skull smashing against the flagstone with a solid crack. He bled out without regaining consciousness.

Bolan suddenly heard raised voices in the vicinity. The stomp of boots grew louder as more of Manolo's crew prepared to put up resistance. He cut across the courtyard, searching for temporary cover. Men were calling to each other in Spanish. They were breaking through the lush banks of flowers and ferns, eager to locate the American interloper. They were Manolo's men, and putting themselves on the line was an expected requisite of their employment.

Bolan raised his Uzi and began blasting from his place of concealment, seeking and finding targets with deadly precision.

Met with sudden silence, no more resistance, Bolan reloaded the Uzi and walked through the hacienda, looking for Raul Manolo. He kicked open doors, checking rooms, and found no one. As he crossed one large, empty room he picked up the sound of voices and the shuffle of feet and saw ahead of him a large, open lounge and beyond that the front door of the house.

He spotted the figure of Manolo, closely followed by his right-hand man, Costa. The Colombians were rushing from the house.

Traversing the wide, sun-lit entrance hall Bolan reached the main door and went through. He picked up the moving figures of Manolo and Costa already on the sloping path that led to the jetty. Heading up the path toward them was the Cuban politician Santos Perez, accompanied by two other men who looked to be confused by the sudden eruption of gunfire.

MANOLO, WITH COSTA and Delgado close behind him, raced forward.

"What has happened?" Perez demanded to know, his face dark with anger. "Do you realize the problems I will face when I return home? Damn you, Raul, if you jeopardize my position…"

Manolo didn't break his stride as he raised the Glock and put two shots into Perez. The Cuban slumped on his knees. Half rising, he raised a pleading hand in Manolo's direction. The Glock cracked a third time, the bullet slamming into Perez's skull, driving him flat on his back.

"Now you don't have to worry about going home," Manolo said as he walked away.

The Cuban officials stood watching, realizing they were as vulnerable as Perez. Confusion showed in their eyes as they faced Manolo.

"Are you going to threaten me, too? Like that idiot back there?"

"We came to talk with the American senator," one of the Cubans said. He made a sweeping gesture. "None of this is what we expected. Santos promised us we would be safe here."

"He was a politician," Manolo said. "So are you. Not so bright if you believed him."

He raised his pistol at the Cubans.

Luis Costa looked over his shoulder and saw the tall, dark-haired man heading in their direction and knew it was Cooper.

"Raul," he said.

Manolo turned. Despite his outer bravado he experienced an unsettling chill at the sight of the big American closing in. He stepped around Costa, raising the Glock, and triggered a pair of shots at the American. He saw his slugs kick up gouts of earth close to Cooper's left foot.

"Go," Costa yelled. "He can't reach us once we get onboard."

The sloping path allowed them to move quickly in the direction of the jetty and the safe haven of *La Perla*. The motor vessel's powerful diesel engines were already running. As Manolo and his two men came into sight a pair of armed men moved to the side of the boat. They raised submachine guns and fired at the pursuing American.

Costa, encouraged by the resistance, turned and raised his own pistol. He gripped it two-handed and aimed, triggering a single shot. He saw the American pause, realizing he had hit the man. A wave of elation swept over him.

"Raul, I hit him."

THE 9 MM SLUG lodged in Bolan's left side, just above his hip. He felt the solid slam of the bullet. The impact threw him off stride but he forced himself to keep moving. Soft tissue absorbed the slug and he was certain it had not hit any organs. Even so he realized it would slow him eventually. Until then he had to keep moving, closing the distance between himself and the men ahead of him.

Bolan steadied the Uzi, bringing it online as Costa made his move to fire again. The Executioner let loose, spitting a stream of 9 mm slugs that found their target. Costa managed to stay upright, his pistol wavering as he attempted to overcome the impact of the slugs his body had absorbed. Bolan's long-honed skills brought the weapon into play again and he held the trigger down, the longer second burst rising to stitch across Costa's chest. Costa went down, bloody and groaning, his body scraping across the rough concrete of the jetty.

With one man down Bolan switched his aim and raked the section of the boat where Manolo's gunmen were positioned. The slugs from the Uzi chopped up polished wood along the side rail, sending raw splinters into the air. As the muzzle of the Uzi rose above the level of the rail, one gunner took slugs in his shoulder, spinning him across the deck. More bullets chunked into the superstructure behind him, shattering one window in the lower cabin section.

Chico Delgado, pistol in his hand, wavered between following hard on Manolo's heels or finding cover. The moment had arrived for him to prove his usefulness, but the sight of Costa being shot had unnerved him. He turned to seek assurance from Manolo. The Colombian kingpin had already moved closer to the boat. In a surge of false bravado Delgado thrust his pistol in the direction of the tall American and triggered a pair of fast, wild shots that did nothing but kick up dust.

Bolan hit Delgado with a short burst that plowed through his chest and devastated the man's heart. Delgado twisted about, crashing down hard on the concrete, his body in spasm.

Bolan ducked behind a neat stack of fuel drums, hearing the sharp clang of slugs hammering the steel of the containers. He used the moment to drop the used magazine and refresh the weapon, snapping back the cocking bolt. He crawled along the line of drums as more gunfire pinned him behind the containers. The odor of raw diesel fuel filled the air as punctured drums sprayed fuel across the jetty.

Bolan reached the end of the line of drums and leaned out to track Raul Manolo as the Colombian trafficker drew level with the short gangway of the boat. There was a faint smile on Manolo's lips as he moved to step onto the gangway. He had reached sanctuary.

The Uzi crackled as Bolan raked the rail section again, driving the gunman there back to cover. The moment he had cleared the rail Bolan pushed to his feet, moved across the jetty and tracked the Uzi in.

"For Maggie Connor," he said quietly.

Bolan hit the trigger and stitched Manolo's lower body and torso. Barely able to support himself on shattered limbs Manolo slipped over the edge of the gangway into the water. He flailed about, the motion of the water covering him, then exposing him. He clawed at the smooth hull of *La Perla*, unable to gain any kind of grip. Blood colored the water around him.

The Executioner turned the Uzi back to the boat, hitting it with short bursts to discourage resistance. His slugs punctured the cabin sides and windows. He used up his magazine and reloaded, keeping up the offensive fire until crew members dropped the fore and aft mooring ropes and *La Perla* slid away from its anchorage. It moved to beyond the Uzi's range, leaving Bolan's solitary figure on the jetty. When he walked to the edge he saw Raul Manolo's body, facedown in the water, close to the wall of the pier.

Bolan felt blood coursing down his blacksuit from the bullet wound in his side. He placed his hand over it, putting pressure on the spot. A wave of nausea swept over him. He used his free hand to pull out the transceiver and thumb the button.

"You there, Loomis?"

The Miami cop answered immediately. "Looking for a ride?"

"Soon as possible, buddy. Bring her around to the east side of the island. You'll see a bay. There are a couple of boats already there. I'll be on the jetty."

"You get a result?"

"Yeah."

"I saw a chopper lift off a while ago," Loomis said.

"That was Ryland and his team. They're clear."

"Cooper, you okay? You don't sound so good."

If Loomis had been there he would have seen Bolan grimace, but all he heard was "It's been a busy few days, Loomis. A busy few days."

"Sit tight," Loomis said. "I'm on my way."

In the water below where Bolan stood, Manolo's body rolled with the tide. It swept in and hit the jetty wall, then floated out a few feet. Bolan watched it dispassionately. His mind was elsewhere, thinking about the body of Maggie Connor and where he had left her wrapped in a sheet near the jungle base in Colombia. He glanced up when he heard the float plane coming in for a landing. He knew he had to call Commander Calberon. He'd tell him Manolo had been taken care of and ask him if he would recover Maggie Connor's body and have it sent back to the U.S. He knew Hal Brognola would see to it she received a proper burial. It was the least they could do for her.

The Executioner always kept his word.

Even to the dead.

Don Pendleton's Mack Bolan

Altered State

Rogue U.S. security forces profit from Afghanistan's heroin trade...

Kabul, Afghanistan, remains a front line within a bureaucratic civil war, where spooks, soldiers, fanatics and narcotics collide in profit and death. Added to the mix are rumors of a heroin operation run by an American private-security firm. With his identity compromised from the start, Mack Bolan is on a mission that threatens to expose the long arm of a traitor.

Available October wherever books are sold.

Or order your copy now by sending your name, address, zip or postal code, along with a check or money order (please do not send cash) for $6.99 for each book ordered ($7.99 in Canada), plus 75¢ postage and handling ($1.00 in Canada), payable to Gold Eagle Books, to:

In the U.S.
Gold Eagle Books
3010 Walden Avenue
P.O. Box 9077
Buffalo, NY 14269-9077

In Canada
Gold Eagle Books
P.O. Box 636
Fort Erie, Ontario
L2A 5X3

Please specify book title with your order.
Canadian residents add applicable federal and provincial taxes.

GOLD EAGLE

www.readgoldeagle.blogspot.com

TAKE 'EM FREE
2 action-packed novels plus a mystery bonus
NO RISK
NO OBLIGATION TO BUY

SPECIAL LIMITED-TIME OFFER
Mail to: Gold Eagle Reader Service

IN U.S.A.: P.O. Box 1867, Buffalo, NY 14240-1867
IN CANADA: P.O. Box 609, Fort Erie, Ontario L2A 5X3

YEAH! Rush me 2 FREE Gold Eagle® novels and my FREE mystery bonus (bonus is worth about $5). If I don't cancel, I will receive 6 hot-off-the-press novels every other month. Bill me at the low price of just $33.44 for each shipment.* That's a savings of over 15% off the combined cover prices and there is NO extra charge for shipping and handling! There is no minimum number of books I must buy. I can always cancel at any time simply by returning a shipment at your cost or by returning any shipping statement marked "cancel." Even if I never buy another book from Gold Eagle, the 2 free books and mystery bonus are mine to keep forever.

166 ADN EYPE   366 ADN EYPQ

Name	(PLEASE PRINT)	
Address		Apt. #
City	State/Prov.	Zip/Postal Code

Signature (if under 18, parent or guardian must sign)

Not valid to current subscribers of Gold Eagle books.
Want to try two free books from another series? Call 1-800-873-8635.

* Terms and prices subject to change without notice. Prices do not include applicable taxes. Sales tax applicable in N.Y. Canadian residents will be charged applicable provincial taxes and GST. Offer not valid in Quebec. This offer is limited to one order per household. All orders subject to approval. Credit or debit balances in a customer's account(s) may be offset by any other outstanding balance owed by or to the customer. Please allow 4 to 6 weeks for delivery. Offer available while quantities last.

Your Privacy: Worldwide Library is committed to protecting your privacy. Our Privacy Policy is available online at www.eHarlequin.com or upon request from the Reader Service. From time to time we make our lists of customers available to reputable third parties who may have a product or service of interest to you. If you would prefer we not share your name and address, please check here. ☐

GE09

JAMES AXLER
DEATH LANDS

Time Castaways

A struggle for tomorrow in the midst of a new reality...

Barely escaping a redoubt hidden in an old aircraft carrier, the companions emerge into the backwater world of Lake Superior's Royal Island, where two rival barons rule mutant-infested land and water. Soon, Ryan finds himself in a death race to stop the secrets of the gateways from becoming open passage to the future's worst enemies.

Available December wherever books are sold.

Or order your copy now by sending your name, address, zip or postal code, along with a check or money order (please do not send cash) for $6.99 for each book ordered ($7.99 in Canada), plus 75¢ postage and handling ($1.00 in Canada), payable to Gold Eagle Books, to:

In the U.S.
Gold Eagle Books
3010 Walden Avenue
P.O. Box 9077
Buffalo, NY 14269-9077

In Canada
Gold Eagle Books
P.O. Box 636
Fort Erie, Ontario
L2A 5X3

GOLD EAGLE

Please specify book title with your order.
Canadian residents add applicable federal and provincial taxes.

www.readgoldeagle.blogspot.com

ROGUE Angel™

AleX Archer
PARADOX

What once may have saved the world could now destroy it...

Archaeologist Annja Creed reluctantly accepts an assignment on behalf of the U.S. government to investigate what is thought to be the remains of Noah's Ark. Annja must escort a group of militants through civil unrest in eastern Turkey, but the impending war is nothing compared to the danger that lies hidden within the team. With lives at stake, Annja has no choice but to protect the innocent. Legend says the Ark once saved mankind...but this time it could kill them all.

Available November wherever books are sold.

GOLD EAGLE®

www.readgoldeagle.blogspot.com